"I think we need to talk." The tone of Mason's voice left no room for objection.

Feeling daring for a change, Rebekah shook her head. "I need to get a good night's sleep so I can be on my way tomorrow."

Mason's eyes blazed, and he looked at her as if she were crazy. He opened his mouth to say something but slammed it shut instead. A muscle flicked angrily in his jaw. Rebekah felt compelled to continue. "I've taken up your time and eaten your food. You've been very kind, and I truly appreciate your hospitality, but I'll be leaving tomorrow."

Mason stalked away then quickly stopped. He pivoted and marched back toward her like a cougar chasing its prey. Rebekah stepped back, the chipped bark of the fallen tree trunk biting into her calves. He leaned into her face. The flickering firelight behind her brought out sparkling flecks of gold in his ebony eyes. His breath warmed her nose, and Rebekah's heart tightened at his intimidating closeness. Mason's steady gaze impaled her. She was suddenly anxious to escape his disturbing presence.

"Kid," he said with cool authority, "you're not goin' anywhere tomorrow."

VICKIE MCDONOUGH is an award-winning author and has lived in Oklahoma and on a kibbutz in Israel. Her inspirational romance credits include novellas in *A Stitch in Time*, *Brides O' the Emerald Isle*, and *Texas Christmas Grooms*. *Sooner or Later* is her first novel. Vickie also writes articles and books reviews. She is a wife of thirty years and mother to four sons. When she's not writing, she enjoys reading, gardening, watching movies, and traveling. Learn more about Vickie's books at www.vickiemcdonough.com.

Sooner or Later

Vickie McDonough

Heartsong Presents

A note from the Author:
I love to hear from my readers! You may correspond with me by writing:

Vickie McDonough
Author Relations
PO Box 719
Uhrichsville, OH 44683

ISBN 1-59310-850-8

SOONER OR LATER

All scripture quotations are taken from the King James Version of the Bible.

All of the characters and events in this book are fictitious. Any resemblance to actual persons, living or dead, or to actual events is purely coincidental.

Our mission is to publish and distribute inspirational products offering exceptional value and biblical encouragement to the masses.

PRINTED IN THE U.S.A.

prologue

April 2, 1889, Southeastern Arkansas

Never in her whole life had Rebekah Bailey done anything so daring, but then, she'd never been this desperate. She peered over her shoulder as she tiptoed toward the barn. In silent support, her shadow marched eerily beside her. The full moon illuminated the rickety A-frame house that had always been her home. The breath she'd been holding came out in a ragged sigh. At least she'd managed to get out of the house without Pa hearing her. But she was far from safe.

Her heartbeat resounded in her ears, and she was certain her neighbors miles away could hear it. Hugging her ancient carpetbag against her chest, she hurried faster.

Sucking in a deep, chilling breath, Rebekah managed to squeeze through the narrow barn door opening without it squeaking. Hopefully, she'd saddle Prince just as quietly, then slip away without waking the man in the house. If not, her world would end—and all her dreams along with it.

The old horse raised his head to peer at her, snorted softly, then ducked back down as if he knew it wasn't time to be awakened. Rebekah set aside her small bundle of possessions. The bulky saddle was always a struggle to lift; but tonight, under stress and fear, she thought it felt extraordinarily heavy. With a grunt, she labored to hoist it onto Prince's back, stealing glances at the barn door lest Pa sneak up on her. Once she had the saddle in place and cinched, she used the leather strings behind the cantle to secure the handles of the old carpetbag that held everything she owned.

"Come on, Prince. You're my champion—my only means of escape," Rebekah whispered to the old gelding as she led him

5

from the stall. His brown ears flicked back and forth as if he were listening intently. "Ride the wind tonight, my prince."

She looped her canteen over the saddle horn, twisted the stirrup around, and inserted her foot. With a quick hop and a soft grunt, she pulled herself onto the horse, ducking her head to avoid smacking it into the hayloft. Rebekah tapped her heels to Prince's side. He raised his head and snorted but didn't move.

"Oh, no. C'mon, boy. Please go." She nudged him again. Prince blew out a soft nicker and mild snort of resignation, then plodded forward.

Rebekah pushed against the barn door with her foot. It swung open on a groan and high-pitched squeal. Body tensing and every nerve fraying, she darted her gaze toward the house. "Oh, please, Lord, don't let Pa hear. Please, God, help me," she pleaded to the moonlit sky.

No shadows moved in the night, and nobody rushed out of the house to stop her. Rebekah clicked twice out the side of her mouth and nudged the horse with her heels. Prince trotted out of the yard and down the road. The *thunk* of his hooves pounding against the hard ground sounded to Rebekah like the mighty roar of a herd of cattle rumbling by.

She blew out a "Shhh," knowing it did no good. Rebekah took another glance at the only home she'd ever known, wishing desperately that things were different. To the north, she saw the shadowy outline of the mighty oak tree standing guard over the graves where her mother and little brother were buried.

Rebekah slowed Prince to a walk and allowed herself a wisp of a moment to bid them good-bye. "I'm sorry, Mama. I can't do what he demands of me," she whispered to the headstones enclosed behind the weathered picket fence. Her stomach churned with the regret of what could have been, and her eyes burned with unshed tears.

If only I could turn back time. Back to when Mama and Davy were alive. Back to when we were a relatively happy family. Back before Pa hated me. If only. . .

A sharp creak in the direction of the house jerked Rebekah from her reverie. With a quick tug on the reins and a nudge of her foot to his flank, she turned Prince west. West toward the open plains and Indian Territory. West toward Denver—and freedom. She prayed it was the last place Pa would think to look for her.

The chanting of tree frogs lent music to her ride, and an owl hooted somewhere in a nearby tree. She used to love the sounds of the night, but now they only reminded her of her pain and loneliness. Hoping to ward off the chill, she tugged her worn cloak around her. The world seemed normal, asleep, as it should in the middle of the night. Rebekah felt anything but normal. Her world had fallen apart this evening with Pa's declaration. Nothing would ever be the same for her. She shivered at the memory.

"I've made a deal with Giles Wilbur," he'd said, grinning with pride. "Swapped you for a side of beef and some moonshine. In the morning, you'll be moving in with him to be his woman." Thoughts of the drunken sloth of a man more than twice her age made her blood run cold. How could Pa expect her to live with Mr. Wilbur without even the sanctity of a wedding? How could he simply swap her like she was something to be bartered? Bile churned in her stomach and burned a path to her throat. Tears blurred her vision and streamed down her cheeks.

She'd never felt so alone. Completely alone—as though not a single person in the world cared for her—but the gentle touch of the wind to her cheek reminded her of the One who never failed. Rebekah turned to her heavenly Father as Prince trotted down the dark road.

"Protect me, Lord—and show me the way. And, Father. . .oh, Father, give me courage for the ride ahead, and strengthen Prince's old bones—"

The faint sound of approaching hoofbeats intruded on Rebekah's prayer.

Oh, no! Pa!

She was certain her heart would jump clear out of her chest. The reins nearly slipped from her trembling hands. Fear of what was behind her overpowered the fear of what was ahead.

Taking a deep, determined breath and a firm grip on the reins, Rebekah dug her heels into Prince's side.

"He-yah," she cried softly.

Prince vaulted into a gallop and raced down the road.

one

"I gots to go, Unca Mathon."

Mason Danfield pushed the black Stetson up on his forehead and turned in his seat to look at his three-year-old niece. "Aw, Katie, not again." She twirled a lock of golden hair around her pudgy finger and stuck out her bottom lip in a little pout. "You're serious? Not just wantin' out of the wagon?"

"I gots to go weal bad." Katie bounced up and down on her quilt in the back of the covered wagon.

Mason glanced past her to where his seven-year-old nephew sat pretending to shoot Indians with his stick rifle. Jimmy rolled his eyes and shook his head. "Don't forget the last time you didn't stop when she said she had to go." He lifted the edge of the patchwork quilt that hung out the back of the wagon, drying in the warm afternoon sun. Jimmy crossed his arms and sighed. "It's not fair. Why couldn't she go on her own quilt?"

Mason pressed his lips together, holding back the chuckle threatening to escape. "Don't worry about it, pardner. There's bound to be some water up ahead. We'll get your quilt washed out soon as we can." Mason pulled back on the long leather reins. "Whoa, Belle, Duke. Hold up there."

The big Conestoga wagon groaned to a stop, and Mason set the brake. Harnesses jingled as the four draft horses stomped and snorted as though they knew it wasn't time to stop yet. Mason jumped down from the tall wagon seat, sending a cloud of dust flying around his boots when he landed. He stretched and twisted to work the kinks out of his back, then scanned the area as he walked around behind the wagon. The tall prairie grass and gently rolling hills were a welcome relief after the steep, green hills of the Ozarks they'd recently crossed.

"Come on, Katie. Make it fast." He waved for her to come

to him. "We've got a long ways to travel today. You, too, pard. You know the rule."

"Yep; when we stop, everyone goes." Jimmy scrambled over the back of the wagon and headed for a group of small trees before Mason had a chance to lift Katie out.

The little cherub stood with her arms reaching toward him. He looked into her angelic face, and his heart clenched the way it always did whenever he thought of Katie's mother. Taking a deep breath, he pushed the memory of his loving sister back into the hidden recesses of his mind. In the future, he would avoid looking directly into the little girl's face. It only made what he was preparing to do all that much harder.

Mason released a heavy breath and lifted his niece over the wagon's tailgate. "Come on, Katie girl, let's go take care of business."

"You sad, Unca Mathon?" Katie's soft hand stroked his cheek, and against his wishes, Mason leaned into the caress.

"Yeah, sugar, I'm a little sad."

"I sad, too. I miss Mama. When's Mama coming back?" Katie's brow crinkled as her thumb eased toward her pink lips.

Mason sighed. "Katie, how many times do I have to explain this? You know your mama and Aunt Annie are in heaven now. They aren't coming back." Mason shifted the little girl to his other arm and chastised himself for being so gruff with her. He sorely missed his wife and sister. How could he not expect a three-year-old to miss her mother just as much? Life was so unfair.

Mason lowered Katie to the ground, and she ran behind an old stump. He looked heavenward and uttered the silent prayer again.

God, how could You let Annie and Danielle die? Why didn't You protect them?

His throat tightened, and his eyes closed against the burning sensation. He was a grown man pushing thirty, yet every time he thought about the death of his wife, Annie, and their unborn child, and his sister, Danielle, he felt like crying. Sobbing, just like Katie did the time she'd lost her favorite doll.

The accident was his fault. *If only I'd—*

"Got somethin' in your eyes, Uncle Mason?" Jimmy asked, skidding to a stop beside him.

Mason rubbed his eyes. It wouldn't help the kids to know he was upset. "Probably just some dust. Looks like it hasn't rained around these parts for quite a while."

Mason knew they were getting low on water, but he didn't want to worry the boy. He hoped they'd come across fresh water soon. They needed it, their stock needed it, and they could all use a bath.

Katie skipped back a moment later and yanked on his trousers to get his attention. "All done," she said, a darling smile creasing the dimples on her cheeks.

"Well then, back in you go." Mason lifted Katie over the wagon's tailgate and set her on her quilt. Her thumb went straight into her mouth. "Grab your dolly and lie down. It's time you took your nap. By the time you wake up, we should be getting close to where we'll make camp for the evening." Katie nodded and curled up with her doll.

Mason helped Jimmy onto the wagon seat then climbed up beside him.

"How much longer until we get to Dad's place?"

"Don't exactly know, Jim. Maybe another week or so."

"That long?" Jimmy whined. His forceful sigh fluttered his long, straight bangs; and he leaned forward on the seat, resting his elbows on his knees.

Mason shook the reins and clucked to the horses. Snorting and pawing, the large animals lurched forward. He glanced out of the corner of his eye and studied his nephew. His features looked so much like his father, Jake's. But the boy had Danielle's dark coloring, just as Mason did. Except for their lightly tanned complexion, with their dark hair and black eyes they could have been mistaken for having Mexican or Indian heritage instead of French. In fact, Mason had been ridiculed many times for being a half-breed, even though his mother was French and his father, a Southern gentleman.

Jake. How would he deal with Danielle's death? Would he even care? His scoundrel of a brother-in-law had chased one dream after another ever since marrying Mason's sister. After moving five different times, Danielle had dug in her heels and refused to leave their home on the outskirts of St. Louis to follow Jake into Indian Territory. Mason exhaled a bitter laugh. The ironic thing was, she might still be alive if only she and the children *had* joined Jake. Then Mason would be missing her for a whole different reason. As it now stood, he missed his sister almost as much as his wife.

For the hundredth time, he wondered if he was doing the right thing. Maybe he should just turn the wagon around and take the kids back to St. Louis, or better still, back to Charleston where his parents still lived on the family's large plantation. But Mason knew he couldn't do that either. There were too many bad memories. He needed to rid himself of all responsibilities. As much as he hated to admit it, that included the children. He couldn't keep them; he needed to cut all ties to his past. Then he'd be free to ride west and forget the wonderful life he once had.

Jimmy tugged on Mason's sleeve, pulling him from his thoughts. He looked down at his nephew. The boy pointed to the trail ahead of them. "Look, there's a rider up ahead. What's the matter with 'im?"

Squinting against the bright glare of the afternoon sun, Mason pulled down the brim of his hat to shade his eyes and scanned the road up ahead. He reached down, picked up his rifle, and laid it across his lap. Mason studied the stranger as they pulled even with him, then scanned the tall prairie grass, hoping the rider wasn't simply a decoy for an ambush. A man could easily hide in the thigh-high grass, but he couldn't conceal a horse. His rigid back relaxed, and his heart slowed its quick pace as he realized the stranger was alone. The small man, hunched over and clinging to his saddle horn, didn't even look up as they approached. Jimmy was right. Something was definitely wrong with the rider.

"Ain't you gonna stop?"

"Nope. I'm not picking up someone who may be sick. Since we're traveling alone, I don't want to chance us catching anything out here on the trail. Besides, the man looks more drunk than sick." Mason wondered what could cause someone to be inebriated in the middle of the afternoon. On second thought, he knew exactly the kind of pain that could drive a man to drink.

He studied the stranger as they rode past him. It surprised him to discover the pale-faced rider was just a skinny boy, probably in his early teens. Surely he wasn't drunk. If not, then he *must* be sick—sick enough he didn't even look up or acknowledge there were others on the trail. They passed the rider, who bounced and reeled with each uneven step his old horse took. In truth, the horse looked to be worse off than the rider.

Wrestling with his conscience, Mason continued down the trail. His hands were full enough with two small children. He didn't need a sick teenager to care for on top of everything else.

Then why do I feel so guilty?

A movement flashed in the corner of his eye, snagging his attention, and he turned to look. Jimmy sat on his knees, backward on the seat, and hung halfway around the side of the wagon so that Mason couldn't even see his head. He reached over, grabbing the tail of Jimmy's faded shirt. "You lean any farther off the wagon seat, boy, and you're gonna fall flat on your noggin. What's so interesting back there?"

"I'm waiting to see if'n that stranger gets up. He fell plumb off his horse."

Turning in his seat, Mason ducked his head, peering through the covered wagon's opening and out the back end. Jimmy was right. The stranger lay flat on his back in the middle of the road. His horse grazed nearby. Mason glanced down at Katie. She slept with her thumb smashed against her bottom lip, blissfully unaware of the dilemma her uncle now faced.

"Whoa, Belle, Duke. Here, pardner, hang on to these while I go back and check on that fellow." Mason handed Jimmy the reins and set the brake. He jumped down, grabbed his rifle, and reached into the back of the wagon, searching the supplies until he found the canteen. As he walked toward the boy, Mason looked heavenward. "Don't I already have enough responsibilities without You dumping another kid on me?" He shook his head. "Folks'll be thinking this is one of those orphan trains."

Balancing against his rifle, Mason knelt beside the boy and studied his face. He had a delicate look about him—city boy, maybe—except his well-worn clothes more resembled something from a farmer's scrap bag. Mason pushed aside the boy's hat and laid his hand against the kid's forehead. At least he didn't have a fever. Maybe he wasn't so sick after all. The boy stirred at Mason's touch.

He set his rifle down on the ground. With a twist of his thumb and forefinger, Mason uncorked the canteen and reached behind the boy to lift him up. His eyes widened and he yanked his hand back as though he'd been stung. The boy lay on top of something that felt like a fat snake—with fur. Cautiously, he lifted the boy's shoulder and rolled him over onto his side. *What in the world?*

Mason jumped to his feet and stepped away. He pushed his hat up his forehead and stood with his hands on his hips, staring at the back of his wagon as he fought to get his ragged breathing under control. How was he going to deal with this? He almost wondered if God were laughing at him. Just when he thought things couldn't get worse, God dropped something like this in his lap.

Mason heard a scuffling noise behind him and spun around. The boy—no, the girl—had managed to sit up. Her well-worn Western hat was back on, and her long braid had disappeared.

Why would a girl be out in the middle of nowhere by herself and dressed in boys' clothing? It didn't make any sense. She must be a runaway.

"Please, c—can I have a drink?"

Her soft, timid voice touched something deep within him, and his anger fell away as if someone had doused him with a bucket of cool creek water. In three steps, he was beside her again. Mason knelt next to the girl. Picking up the canteen, he chastened himself for dropping it earlier and allowing some of the precious liquid to seep out.

The girl's small, trembling hands reached for the canteen. She barely had enough energy to hold it, but she managed to get it to her lips. She guzzled the water and choked from the effort. Liquid droplets trickled over her full lips and down her sun-kissed chin.

Mason wanted to tell her to stop wasting the water, but instead he looked toward the horizon, his jaw clenched. He lifted his hat and swiped at the line of sweat on his forehead, then sucked in a deep breath and let it out through his nose.

How could I have mistaken her for a boy?

❧

Rebekah was amazed she'd made it so far. Right now she was so exhausted and famished, she could barely hold her head up. Thank the Lord, the tall cowboy had materialized just when she thought she could go no farther. She closed her eyes and licked the water from her dry, leathery lips, savoring the life-sustaining moisture. Almost two days without water and food had nearly done her in.

Has water ever tasted so good?

Licking her lips, Rebekah looked around the unfamiliar countryside. Where was she now? Still in Arkansas? Missouri, maybe? The dirt had a strange orange tint to it, and the gently rolling hills reminded her of a pan of yeast rolls rising on the stove. Clusters of trees stood here and there, as if afraid to face the ever-changing weather of the plains alone. Knee-high prairie grass danced and swished on the soft spring breeze. This place was so different from the forested woods of her home.

Home.

She longed for it, dreamed about it, but knew she no longer had a home. Her pa had seen to that. But then, he wasn't really her pa either. Rebekah shook her head and blinked back the burning sensation in her eyes. *How could I have been so naive all those years?*

She tilted her head to look up at the tall cowboy, ignoring the pain it caused. He kicked a tuft of grass and sent it sailing through the air. The man glanced at her and then looked at a covered wagon stopped on the road. His hands rested in his back pockets, and he heaved a loud sigh. He didn't seem happy to be helping her.

Well, she only needed his help a little. It had been foolish of her to leave home with so few provisions, but then, she'd left in a hurry. If only this man could spare some food and water, she'd be on her way.

Suddenly he turned back toward her. His face disappeared in the glare of the noonday sun. "Where you headed, kid?"

"Um. . .Denver." Her scratchy voice sounded foreign to her.

"Denver! On that old thing?" He raised his arm and pointed at Prince. "You'd never make it. And where's your supplies? You don't even have any saddlebags."

Rebekah leaned back, cringing at the disapproval in his voice. What did it matter to him if she rode a horse older than herself and she was ill-prepared for a long journey? Okay, so it mattered if she had to beg food and water from him, but he had no idea how desperate she'd been to get away.

Biting back a retort, Rebekah took another drink from the canteen, then set it down on the dusty road. Her vision had cleared, though her head still throbbed. Probably from too much sun and not enough food, she told herself. She didn't know if her legs would hold her, but she couldn't sit in the middle of the trail all day. Forget the food. If she could just get back on her horse, she could get away from the man's glaring gaze. Easing onto her knees, with her hands firmly anchored in the dirt, she pushed her hind end in the air and straightened her legs. Very unladylike. But then, he didn't know she was a woman.

Her whole body wobbled. Her arms trembled as she tried to push to a stand. She was stuck—not enough strength to get up and too much stubbornness to sit back down. Rebekah imagined she must look like a newborn foal trying out its legs for the first time.

"Here, let me help." A deep voice rumbled in her ear the same moment she felt two warm hands on her waist.

Rebekah stiffened. She turned her head back to see the man's face. She blinked. A pair of the blackest eyes she'd ever seen glared at her.

Why was he so upset with her? Could simply helping a stranger in need cause him to lose his temper? Or maybe he always scowled. Well, she hadn't ridden all this way and left her home just to fall prey to another man like Pa—or Giles Wilbur. She tried to shrug away from the man's hands; instead she felt her body being pulled upright.

The cowboy lifted her up like she was nothing but a five-pound sack of flour and set her on her feet. Immediately her legs buckled. How dare they betray her in her moment of need! Against her wishes, Rebekah clung to the man's waist, her face pressed against his solid chest. She summoned every ounce of energy within her exhausted frame and forced her body upward.

A group of crows floating lazily in the sky cawed as if mocking her. She thought she heard the man gasp—or was he laughing at her? The sky darkened suddenly when a thick cloud floated in front of the sun. Was it raining? She groaned. The last thing she needed was rain. It took her a moment to comprehend that the moisture on her cheeks wasn't from an afternoon shower; it was tears.

No! she chided herself. She couldn't be crying. She just couldn't. She wouldn't cry now—not after all she'd been through.

Rebekah's head sagged heavily, and her tears seemed to have a mind of their own. Blinking, she struggled to dam the tears and focus on her surroundings. She was determined not to show weakness, but her body had other ideas. Her legs shook, her arms trembled, and her head throbbed as if a whole flock of crows were nesting there. Unwillingly, she sagged against the man.

Why is the sky so dark? She tried to ask him that very question, but the words wouldn't form on her thick tongue. Any second now, her head was sure to explode like a stick of dynamite with a short, burning fuse. Rebekah forced herself to lean back so she could look at the man's face, but it swirled into a dark mass and merged into the growing blackness.

"Hey! Hold on now," she thought she heard him say. Then the deep voice faded away into the shadowy abyss.

two

Mason hoisted the young woman into his arms and started toward the wagon. "All right. I can take a hint!" he shouted to the sky.

Jimmy peered, wide-eyed, out the wagon opening. "Wha'cha gonna do, Uncle Mason?"

That was a good question. What *was* he going to do? Taking on a sick girl certainly wasn't in his plans. Mason shook his head. "Never mind. Just climb down and get that horse. Tie him to the back of the wagon—and fetch the canteen and my rifle."

Jimmy scampered over the wagon's tailgate and dropped to the ground. "Are we gonna keep that boy? What's wrong with him?"

"Shhh! You're going to wake Katie with all your chatter," Mason hissed. "And I don't know what's wrong yet." He looked into the pale, dirt-smudged, feminine face and studied the woman's soft features. She wasn't beautiful, but she wasn't exactly hard on the eyes either.

He'd nearly come undone when those vulnerable blue eyes, filled with tears, stared up at him. What was it about a female's tears that moved him so? Maybe it was a result of having so many strong women in his life. He'd known the few times he'd seen them crying that things were bad—real bad. He hadn't missed the sudden flash of stubbornness in the girl's countenance when she tried to stand without his help. But despite her determination, she was obviously too weak.

What had happened to her? Why was she out here alone? Against his will, Mason felt a sudden surge of protectiveness. No harm would come to her while she was in his care.

Carefully, he lifted the limp girl over his shoulder, then

climbed into the back of the wagon. Thankfully, Katie's little body was curled against the side of the wagon instead of being all sprawled out as usual.

Mason eased down his bundle onto the quilt next to Katie, then knelt beside her. The girl's old felt hat flopped over her face. He picked it up, tossing it aside. Her long braid coiled around her shoulder and rested against her arm. Wisps of soft, brown hair escaped her braid, feathering her cheeks. Now that he knew she was a female, Mason decided she must be older than he'd first thought—late teens, maybe. Still, she had no business traveling alone, unprepared and unprotected.

Katie would enjoy having another female around. Mason shook his head. Having a young woman around wasn't part of his plan. Hopefully, when the girl came to, he could help her get back to her family without deviating from his journey for too long.

Mason pulled his bandanna from his neck and gently wiped at the smudged dirt trails on the woman's pale cheek. He'd need water to get the dirt off, but since he was so low on drinking water, he'd been rationing it, not using any of the precious liquid for cleaning. All he had right now was spit, and he doubted the woman would take kindly to his cleaning her face with that.

"Hey, Uncle Mason," Jimmy said through the back of the wagon in a loud whisper. "Can I ride on this horse instead of in the wagon?"

Mason glanced over the wagon's tailgate and eyed the pitiful beast, wondering how far it had carried its cargo. The bony animal's ribs stuck out, causing Mason to speculate how its saddle had stayed on. The poor creature should have been put out to pasture years ago. He shook his head, and Jimmy's bright smile faded. "Better wait till it's had some water. We don't know how long they've been traveling."

"Oh, okay." With disappointment marring his face, Jimmy slid off the horse and tied it to the back of the wagon. "Here's the canteen and rifle."

Stretching tall, Jimmy barely reached over the top of the tailgate. Mason grabbed both items, noticing how Jimmy's shoulders slumped as he turned and patted the old horse's withers. Mason sighed. He'd planned on getting Jimmy a small horse on his last birthday, but then the accident had happened—and in that instant, everything changed.

Stop it! Move on.

Yeah, move on, he urged himself again. But he couldn't bring himself to do so. He just couldn't. He missed Annie. He wanted her back. He wanted their child. But Annie wouldn't have wanted him to grieve so long, and to this extent. She'd made him promise if anything happened to her that he'd marry again. *What a dumb promise.* As if any woman could ever have a place in his heart after Annie.

"No, Pa—don't." The woman's cry jolted Mason back to the present.

A dull *thud* echoed through the wagon as she kicked a crate with the heel of her worn boot. He glanced at Katie, afraid the young woman's thrashing and crying out would wake her. Katie exhaled a loud breath and turned onto her side but thankfully didn't awaken. With a quick tug, Mason removed the girl's boots and set them near the tailgate.

"Shhh! It's okay." Mason reached out and patted the girl's arm.

She pulled away at his touch. Her forehead gleamed with sweat. Tears running from the corner of her eye formed a tiny river as they cut a trail through the dirt on her sunburned cheeks.

"No, Pa. I—I promise." Anguish contorted her countenance. "I'll be good."

Moved by her tears, Mason went against his own rule and grabbed the canteen. He moistened his bandanna, then ran the damp cloth over the woman's forehead. What had her pa done to her? He shivered at the thought of what the young woman might have endured.

"Please don't," she mumbled.

"Shhh. Hush now, you're all right," he whispered, smoothing her damp hair out of her face. At the sound of his voice,
she relaxed and stopped her thrashing. The tears slowed
to a single drop, clinging stubbornly to her dark lashes.
Mason dabbed at it, then gently wiped her face. Her warm,
sun-kissed cheeks were soft in spite of the layer of dust.
Almost against his will, he felt his heart going out to her. He
turned and looked out the back of the wagon to the bright
summer sky.

*Well, if I can take care of two kids who aren't mine, I can take
care of a third.*

❧

Rebekah lay still, trying to make sense of her surroundings.
She could hear the soft cadence of nearby voices. A deep
baritone, a youthful alto, and a soft soprano wafted on the
night like a melody, as a chorus of crickets and cicadas
strummed the background music. Lulled by the sounds of
peace and contentment, she thought of home and happier
times. Of nights on the front porch swing with her mother,
listening to a similar string of players. She wanted to drift
back to sleep and stay on the porch with her mom forever;
then a child's innocent giggle momentarily drowned out the
night orchestra and called her back to the present.

Where am I?

In the orange glow of the fading sunlight, she could make
out the rounded canopy of a covered wagon. She fingered
the quilt beneath her. It felt so good to lie on something soft
instead of the cold, hard ground. How long had it been since
she left home? Five days?

Her nose twitched. Rebekah caught a whiff of something
that smelled like fried chicken, and her stomach grumbled
in response. Her last decent meal had been the day she left
home. She'd served crispy fried chicken that night—and
mashed potatoes with blobs of melted butter, flaky biscuits,
and fresh corn on the cob. Saliva moistened her tongue. That
was almost a week ago. The chicken and biscuits she'd taken

with her when she fled her childhood home were gone days ago. A few overripe peaches had been her only source of nourishment since then. No wonder she was so weak.

The murmur of voices floated in again on the warm evening breeze. She listened carefully. The deep, rumbling voice, thick with a smooth Southern drawl, sounded vaguely familiar. The memory of the black-eyed man glaring at her stole the breath right out of her lungs. *Could this be his wagon?* She jerked upright. Pain resonated through her head from the swift movement.

A rustling at the end of the wagon drew her attention. Two small hands grabbed the back edge of the wagon, and a dark head appeared. A pair of black eyes, a smaller version than the one in her memory, stared wide-eyed at her.

"He's awake! Uncle Mason, he's awake." And just that fast, the boy was gone.

Rebekah glanced around for her hat. Quickly she coiled her braid and stuffed it inside, then smashed the hat onto her head. Near the back end of the wagon, she spied her boots. She crawled over to them, staring out the wagon opening as she moved. No one was within her line of sight.

Rebekah glanced down and grabbed a boot. Hearing a scuffling noise, she glanced up. Less than two feet away were the ebony eyes that haunted her memory. She gasped and leaned back. The man's black eyes twinkled momentarily and then dulled.

"Well now, 'bout time you woke up. Thought maybe you'd sleep clean through the night. You hungry, kid?"

Rebekah listened to his voice—a voice smoother than melted butter on warm biscuits. From his accent, she surmised he was from the Deep South—Alabama, maybe. She didn't care; she just liked the sound of it. His eyes didn't seem so threatening now, but he still managed to make her gut contract.

Thank You, Lord, for the boy. At least I'm not alone with this intimidating stranger.

Was the boy his son? It seemed reasonable. They had the same eyes. The same head of dark hair. No, he called him Uncle—Mike or something. Again her stomach complained about its empty state. She pressed her hand to her belly as quickly as she could to muffle the sound.

The man cleared his throat, his lips tilted in an amused smirk. "Sounds like you're hungry to me."

Rebekah realized she'd been staring. Intimidating or not, he was quite handsome, especially with several days' growth of black whiskers that gave him a rugged look. She felt her cheeks warming and looked away.

"Um. . .well, yes. I'm hungry."

"Then get yourself on down here fore Jimmy finishes off the roasted rabbit."

Rebekah's heart sank. Rabbit. Not chicken. Oh, well, any food would taste good. She shouldn't complain. Her stomach growled deep and low as if to agree.

She pulled on her boots, stood slowly, then hiked her leg over the back of the wagon. Straddling the tailgate, she set her foot down on a section of wood jutting out the back end. The wagon swirled, fading to darkness then back to light. She paused to catch her balance. The man's hands captured her waist, and warmth radiated up her side. Rebekah froze. *Does he know I'm a woman? Why else would he help me down?*

Straddling the tailgate, she turned, glaring at the man. "I can get down by myself."

"Beggin' your pardon, but you already collapsed in my arms once today. I'm just trying to prevent that from happenin' again. You *are* still weak, you know."

Rebekah felt sure he spat out each individual word on purpose just to emphasize his point. Heat marched up her cheeks. *Collapsed in his arms? What could he be talking about?* Turning away from his penetrating stare, she started to hike her other leg over the side, but the ground below her whirled as if someone had set it in motion. If she didn't know better, she might have believed the solid ground beneath her had turned to water. She clutched the top of the tailgate with a white-knuckled grip. With great resolve she fought the dizziness and weakness. She wouldn't give him the satisfaction of being right.

Regaining her equilibrium, she hoisted her leg over the tailgate and was maneuvering quite well when her pants snagged on the head of a protruding nail. She tugged slightly but couldn't free herself. With a sigh of frustration, she gave her britches a quick yank. The sound of ripping fabric hit her ears the same second her pant leg tore free. The momentum forced her other foot off the wooden ledge, and Rebekah dove over the tailgate—straight into the stranger's arms.

She grabbed hold of the man's shoulders to keep from falling farther. Then she secured her hat just before it slipped off. Rebekah quickly realized she needn't worry about falling. His strong arms held her securely against his solid chest; and his breath, warm on her cheek, still carried the faint hint of roasted rabbit. In spite of her embarrassment and the fact that she'd never been this close to a man before in her whole life, his arms felt entirely too comfortable—too secure.

Rebekah was so mortified she couldn't bring herself to look into his face for fear of seeing a satisfied grin. She'd fallen just like he'd said. Only it wasn't from being weak; it was merely a simple accident that had tripped her up. But she was sure he wouldn't believe her if she tried to explain.

When he stepped back and turned toward the campfire, Rebekah noticed the boy and a younger girl staring at them. The man started toward the campfire, and she realized he wasn't going to set her down. She smacked his rock-hard chest with her open hand. "Put me down," she ordered. "I'm fine."

"Uh-huh. If you're fine, how come I caught you tumbling through the air like a shot goose?"

Of all the nerve. Insufferable man!

Oompf! He hastily deposited her on a rotting tree stump. Then he sat down on the gnarled tree trunk that lay on the ground beside her. Thinking about what creatures might be nesting in such an old, decaying stump caused Rebekah to cringe. There could be spiders, maggots, and all kinds of critters, maybe even snakes. That thought had her on her feet in seconds. Ready to investigate what other creatures might be lurking there, she spun around, and the trunk suddenly blurred. It formed and then faded as if she were looking at it through a fog. Instantly she felt the man by her side, his steadying hand warming her shoulder.

"Sit down before you fall down."

Fine. I'll sit down, but only so I don't end up in your arms again. She pointed to the trunk, and he guided her, offering his silent support until she sat down. With her elbows on her knees, Rebekah rested her throbbing head in her hands.

After a few moments of someone shuffling around, she looked up to see the man standing in front of her with a bowl of roasted rabbit and a biscuit. Her stomach cried, *Hurry!* and she accepted the bowl.

"Thank you."

"Don't mention it."

She tore into the meat, ignoring the manners her mother had drilled into her. When the meat was gone, she licked the remaining juice off the bones. Besides, boys didn't have to eat in a ladylike manner; and if she was going to pass herself off as one, she'd have to remember that. The hard biscuit crunched as she chewed it, but she didn't care. It tasted wonderful.

"Uncle Mason don't let me wear my hat when *I* eat," the boy commented, staring at her hat.

She gulped. Seemed there were other things a boy should do. Like be a gentleman, maybe. She just hoped the man wouldn't come yank her hat from her head. She wasn't ready to share her secret.

"Jimmy! That's no way to talk to a guest," the man scolded.

Rebekah sighed with relief and looked at him. Mason. It was a nice name for such an overbearing man. She glanced at Jimmy. His head hung down, and he toed circles in the dirt.

"Sorry," he mumbled without looking up.

So Mason was Jimmy's uncle. Rebekah glanced at the little girl—a darling angel staring at her with wide, dark blue eyes. She held up a ragged cloth doll, whose braided yellow hair hung precariously by several loose threads. "This is Molly," she said.

Rebekah considered how a boy might answer. They'd probably give a disinterested smile, shrug, and say something like, "That's nice"; but she was interested, and she wanted to talk to the child. She'd never had the chance to be around little girls much. "Molly's very pretty. What's your name?"

"Katie. I'm fwee."

Rebekah smiled. "You're three? My, you're a big girl, aren't you?"

Smiling, Katie nodded, and charming dimples dented her chubby cheeks. Rebekah studied the little girl. Her worn dress had seen better days. Her face was covered in what looked like a layer of dirt mixed most likely with grease from the rabbit she'd just eaten. Was she Mason's niece—or maybe his daughter? And why wasn't there a woman around? Jimmy's mom or Mason's wife—if he had one. She glanced around once more, waiting for a woman to appear, but she somehow knew there wasn't one coming.

Savoring the salty dryness of the last of her biscuit, she studied Mason. He squatted next to the fire, stirring the ashes with a stick. The campfire snapped and popped as if complaining about the disturbance. Several days' growth of dark whiskers shadowed Mason's face. Rebekah wondered what he looked like without a beard. His stature was all man—tall, broad-shouldered, strong. She wondered if he carried Indian or Mexican blood, though his tan complexion didn't carry the reddish tint she figured a man of that heritage would. Those black eyes, probing like a lantern at midnight, had nearly penetrated her fragile disguise. The biscuit churned in her stomach. Jimmy's uncle certainly was an appealing man—too much so for her own good.

Would she be safe if she confessed she was a woman? She'd heard stories about what happened to women who traveled alone. That's why she'd disguised herself in her brother's clothes. She hoped to pass for a teenage boy, hoped to waylay unwanted attention. What would Mason do if he knew the truth? Would he be sympathetic?

Rebekah looked up. Her gaze locked with Mason's. Her heart froze. Flickering shadows from the campfire danced across his face. Flames popped, and a hundred tiny embers sprinkled the air like flittering fireflies on the evening hillside. From under half-lowered lids, he stared at her. His glare burned through her. Disconcerted, she crossed her arms and pointedly looked away.

What have I done to upset him?

three

Was he wrong to be cautious? Maybe he should just give the girl some food and water and send her on her way. Mason stood and shoved his hands into his back pockets as he continued to stare into the flickering flames. No. He couldn't do that, even if she wasn't being completely honest with him. He exhaled a heavy breath. Sometimes he hated being chivalrous and caring, but it was his nature.

Mason wondered how much time would pass before the girl trusted him enough to reveal her identity. He always tried hard to give people the benefit of the doubt, but he couldn't stomach a liar or deceiver. A shiver charged up his spine as his thoughts flashed back to his youth, when his father had beaten him whenever he told a lie. Sometime when he was about nine years old, Mason had figured out honesty was a lot less painful than dishonesty. As a boy, he'd entertained ideas of running away from home every time his domineering father took him to the woodshed. Could her father have beaten her? He thought back to her soft cries in the wagon. Was that why she was on the road alone?

He walked away from the heat of the fire. The toe of his boot snagged on a rock, and Mason stumbled, nearly losing his balance. Irritated, he picked up the offending stone with a growl and threw it into the surrounding darkness. He peeked back to see if the woman was watching, but thankfully she was staring into the fire. She looked so scruffy and pitiful.

All his life he'd been rescuing animals and standing up for the smaller kids who were picked on by bullies. Mason wanted to help the woman, but how could he if she wasn't honest with him? He turned back toward the fire.

"What's your name?" Katie asked her.

Something akin to panic dashed across the woman's face. "Re. . .uh. . .RJ."

"That's a funny name." Katie giggled. "How olds are you?"

Mason opened his mouth to scold Katie for her precocious questions, but he decided he'd rather hear RJ's response.

The woman's lips tilted in a melancholy smile. "A lot older than you, sweetie."

Sweetie. At least she was kind to the kids. He'd give her that much. But could RJ be her real initials—or was that just another lie? Never in all his life had he heard of a woman who went only by initials. Mason shook his head.

The moon peeked out from behind a cloud, signaling the lateness of the hour. He watched another cloud meander across the sky to cover the moon, and he sighed. Every night Katie gave him trouble at bedtime. He hoped tonight would be different. "Jimmy, Katie, time for y'all to turn in."

"What am I gonna sleep on?" Jimmy asked.

"Ain't you got a bed?" Mason replied.

"Katie wet on my quilt, remember?"

Mason lifted his hat from his head and ran his hands through his hair. He remembered. He hoped they'd find water soon so they could wash Jimmy's quilt and restock their water barrels. Given the distance they'd traveled without finding fresh water, he'd even considered praying. But his praying days ended when God let Annie and their unborn child die. Why hadn't God prevented it? He could have but He hadn't. As far as Mason was concerned, he had no place in his life for a God who killed women and children.

He looked at Jimmy. "Sorry, pardner, you're gonna have to sleep on your quilt until we can get it washed."

"Oh, great!" Jimmy threw Katie a dirty look and stomped off toward the wagon.

Mason plucked a stem of grass and twirled it between his fingers. He studied Jimmy's back as the boy moved away. Normally all three of them slept together in the wagon, but it wouldn't be proper to make RJ sleep outside, especially in her weakened condition. Mason flicked the grass stem out into the darkening shadows. The girl hadn't been there for a whole day, and she was already forcing changes.

"Jimmy," Mason called. The boy stopped and swirled around. "Throw your quilt under the wagon. We'll sleep out tonight."

The lad's countenance instantly changed. "Woo-hoo!" he yelled. Jimmy punched the air with his fist and burst into a jog toward the wagon. Mason couldn't help smiling. He couldn't begin to count the number of times Jimmy had begged to sleep outside, but he'd always refused the boy since Katie was afraid to sleep alone.

RJ smiled, picked up the canteen, then poured some water into a tin cup. She snapped the cork into the canteen and sipped the water as she stared into the campfire. Mason wanted to talk with her and find out where she'd come from, but first he had to deal with Katie, whose eyes already swam with unshed tears.

"I don't wanna thleep in the wagon by myself. I–I'm scared." The firelight brightened the tears streaming down Katie's cheeks. She hugged Molly tight against her chest.

Mason strode over and knelt beside her. Stroking her silky hair, he pulled her to his chest. "Shhh, sugar. You won't be alone. RJ will be sleeping with you."

Peering past Katie, Mason noticed RJ's head jerk up. He read the probing question in her eyes. He wanted to answer her. *Yes, I know you've been lying. Yes, I know you're a woman.* But he refrained.

Katie pushed away and sat up, rubbing her sleeve across her nose. "Weally?"

"Really." Mason smiled at her excitement. "And I'll tell you what. How about if you go to sleep under the wagon with Jimmy, and later on I'll put you inside?"

Katie squealed and wrapped her arms around Mason's neck. He loved her little-girl hugs and wet, slobbery kisses.

"Come on, sugar," he said, lifting her into the air. "Let's wash up and I'll tuck you in."

❧

Rebekah watched Mason carry Katie to the wagon. When he tossed her up and caught her, the girl's childish squeals rent the night air. He set Katie down and pulled out a canteen from the back of the wagon, then moistened the edge of his shirt and wiped Katie's face. He replaced the canteen, pulled Katie's dress off, and reached in the back of the wagon, retrieving a small ivory-colored nightgown. Mason slipped it over Katie's head, and she scooted under the wagon. Mason knelt beside her. Rebekah heard the murmur of the children's voices and surmised they must be praying.

Looking toward the night sky, Rebekah marveled again at God's handiwork. Back home, the forest of trees blocked out most of the stars, but here the sky sparkled with hundreds of twinkling diamonds. The soothing glow of the moon rising over the eastern sky, to say nothing of her full stomach, lulled her into a contented state. For the first time in a week, she wasn't in a frantic race away from home, worried about finding something to eat, or fearful for her safety.

She glanced at Mason. Even though the man barely spoke to her and continually glared at her, she felt safe with him. Just as quickly as the thought came, it was replaced. Irritation seeped in as Rebekah wondered how Mason could allow a total stranger to sleep in the wagon with Katie, especially if he thought she was a boy. It didn't make any sense. Did he discern she wasn't a threat? But how could he know for sure? And why would he take a chance?

The thought angered her so that she couldn't sit still. She bounced to her feet, instantly sorry for her sudden movement. Reaching down, she steadied herself on the tree stump.

"Just what do you think you're doing?" Mason's voice snapped behind her.

The nearness of his voice startled her. Rebekah gasped and whirled around. She pressed her palm to her chest, hoping to steady her racing heart, and flung out her other arm for balance. Strong hands grabbed her shoulders, steadying her.

How could a man so big walk so quietly?

"I—I need to tend to my horse and get my blanket." Too exhausted to look into his glaring eyes again, Rebekah stared at a blue button on Mason's plaid shirt. The top edge of his chest pocket flopped over in a frayed triangle where the corner had come unstitched. There was no doubt this motley trio could use a woman's touch. Too bad she would be leaving for Denver after everyone fell asleep.

The pungent scent of smoke and dust permeated Mason's shirt. Rather than finding the odor repulsive, Rebekah had to fight off the desire to lean against his solid torso. For the first time in her life, she found herself attracted to a man.

Why did it have to be this one?

"I already took care of that pitiful beast."

Rebekah sucked in a breath and shoved Mason in the chest. "Prince isn't pitiful. He saved my life. I'd have never made it this far without him."

Mason spewed out a noise that sounded half-laugh and half-snort. "How old is that horse, anyway? Twenty-five years?"

Rebekah narrowed her eyes at Mason's offensive comment. She nibbled at a piece of dried skin on her sun-scorched lips. There was no way she would tell this insufferable man that her horse was probably closer to thirty. In fact, Prince was probably older than Mason. As long as Rebekah could remember, her mother had owned Prince.

"I'm going to turn in," she said, purposefully ignoring his question. She tilted her nose toward the stars.

"I think we need to talk." The tone of Mason's voice left no room for objection.

Feeling daring for a change, Rebekah shook her head. "I need to get a good night's sleep so I can be on my way tomorrow."

Mason's eyes blazed, and he looked at her as if she were crazy. He opened his mouth to say something but slammed it shut instead. A muscle flicked angrily in his jaw. Rebekah felt compelled to continue. "I've taken up your time and eaten your food. You've been very kind, and I truly appreciate your hospitality, but I'll be leaving tomorrow."

Mason stalked away then quickly stopped. He pivoted and marched back toward her like a cougar chasing its prey. Rebekah stepped back, the chipped bark of the fallen tree trunk biting into her calves. He leaned into her face. The flickering firelight behind her brought out sparkling flecks of gold in his ebony eyes. His breath warmed her nose, and Rebekah's heart tightened at his intimidating closeness. Mason's steady gaze impaled her. She was suddenly anxious to escape his disturbing presence.

"Kid," he said with cool authority, "you're not goin' anywhere tomorrow."

≈

Rebekah's tears slowed to a mere dribble. Her throat and nose felt thick from her lengthy cry. Though she lay in the back of the wagon next to Katie, she'd never felt so alone. Even her prayers seemed to go no further than the top of the wagon's canvas canopy.

Her emotions bounced from rage to fear and loneliness then back to rage. How could she have been attracted to that beast? How could Mason think he could keep her from leaving? So what if her horse was old? Prince had gotten her this far, and he would get her all the way to Denver. She hadn't run away from Pa simply to fall prey to another tyrant. No. She had to leave tonight.

All her life, Rebekah's mother had told her stories about her hometown. The snowcapped mountains she spoke of had beckoned Rebekah as a child, and when she fled from Pa, it seemed only natural to head for Denver.

Denver was far enough away that Giles Wilbur or her pa wouldn't find her—she hoped. Rebekah still thought of Curtis Bailey as her pa, even though she now knew the truth. The man had raised her and she carried his name, after all. But knowing the truth answered a lot of her questions. How many times had Rebekah asked her mother why she had blue eyes when her pa, ma, and brother all had brown eyes? Now she knew why Curtis—that's what she'd call him from now on—treated Davy so much better than he'd ever treated her. Davy was his true son, and she was merely the unwanted stepchild.

Tears blurred her vision of the moon again. *Oh, Lord, why did You let Ma and Davy die?* Doc said it was influenza. If only Curtis had been home instead of out hunting. Rebekah wouldn't leave her sick mother and brother to go for the doctor. What if she had? Would they still be alive?

Once again, the Bible verse from Ecclesiastes flittered through her mind. *"To every thing there is a season, and a time to every purpose under the heaven: a time to be born, and a time to die."* Was this God's way of telling her it was time for Ma and Davy to die? But why? Davy had filled her life with such joy. He'd only been a few years older than Jimmy when he died. Rebekah wanted so much to be angry with God, but she couldn't. She didn't understand, but still, she wouldn't blame God. Things happened. Life was hard. Right now God was the only constant in her life, her only anchor in a terrifying storm.

A flash of Giles Wilbur's dirty, unshaven face flashed across her mind, sending shivers racing down her spine. The food warming her stomach threatened to come back up as she realized how close she'd come to becoming his wife. How could Curtis consider selling her—and to a horrible man like Giles Wilbur? A man older than himself. His drinking buddy, no less.

Rebekah wiped her nose on her sleeve and breathed a prayer of thanks for her escape. The rider she had thought was Curtis thankfully had turned out to be a stranger. Rebekah had turned Prince off the road the night of her escape and hidden in a cluster of trees while the rider approached and rode past. God had been with her that night and in the days that followed. He would be with her tonight as she made another escape.

It would have been nice to travel under the protection of a man and to enjoy the children's company, but she couldn't afford to dawdle. Even in his old age, Prince moved much faster than the heavy wagon with its cumbersome load. Who knew how close Curtis was behind her? She couldn't give him time to catch up to her. She had to keep moving—and fast. No, this wagon would be much too slow. Her only chance was alone on horseback. God would give Prince the strength he needed to get her to Denver.

"Kid, you're not goin' anywhere tomorrow." Mason's words reverberated in Rebekah's mind like the steady drip of rain on a tin roof.

How dare he think he can keep me here against my will! Come morning, we'll just see about that.

Rebekah flipped onto her side, listening to Katie's steady breathing and the occasional sucking noise she made with her tongue against her thumb. A smile creased Rebekah's mouth. She would miss Katie's sweet smile. There was no guile in her, just innocent childishness. What would it be like to be Katie's mother? To feel her chubby arms wrapped lovingly around her neck as Katie had wrapped them around Mason's? For a moment, Rebekah envied him.

"Mama," Katie called in her sleep.

"Shhh, sweetie, it's okay," she whispered. Reaching out in the darkness, she found Katie's arm and patted it gently.

As if she'd been hit by lightning, Rebekah wondered if this young girl and she shared the same loss. A heaviness centered in her chest. Yes, she would miss Katie. Rebekah choked back a sob.

Katie rolled over in her sleep, and the warmth of her body pressed against Rebekah's stomach. The trust she exuded in her sleep made Rebekah's heart ache even more. If only things were different, she'd love to stay and get to know Katie and Jimmy better. She reached out and pulled Katie against her chest, then placed a gentle kiss on the girl's silky hair.

Mason's voice, soft and deep, filtered through her mind. He

called Katie "sugar"—except it sounded more like "suguh." A girl could fall in love with his slow Southern drawl. In fact, most of the words he uttered that ended in *er* sounded more like they ended in *ah*. *Nevah*. *Ovah*. A smile tugged at the corner of her mouth. But in the next instant, his flashing obsidian eyes and clipped words branded her mind.

"Kid, you're not goin' anywhere."

"And just who does he think he is?" she whispered to the canvas above her. "God?" Rebekah knew full well Mason wasn't God, which cleared her to be angrier with him. No, she couldn't be angry with God, but she certainly could be angry with the man who seemed bent on holding her against her will. She hugged Katie tighter, as if receiving strength from the little girl. The corner of Rebekah's mouth tilted into a smile and her eyes narrowed.

"We'll just see who's not going anywhere tomorrow, Mr. High-and-Mighty."

☙

Mason flipped onto his side, trying to get comfortable on the hard ground. His head rested against RJ's saddle. The scent of leather, a smell he'd always loved, reminded him of his boyhood home and the huge stables filled with saddles and all manner of horse paraphernalia. It was one of only a handful of pleasant memories he had of his childhood.

His father, Colonel Charles Danfield of the Confederate army, had always demanded strict discipline, especially of Mason, his only son. Mason never doubted the colonel loved him, but he had a unique way of showing it.

The soft sobbing above him shredded his heart. He hadn't meant to be so gruff with RJ. The woman had a way of setting him off with her stubborn foolishness. Not to mention her deception. But there was no doubt in his mind that she hadn't been lying when she cried out while unconscious. Mason knew he should have been gentler with her, considering how much she'd been through and how weak she was. He wanted to go find her father and knock some sense into the man. What had the man done to her?

RJ seemed like a wet kitten someone had left out in a cold rain. Mason wanted to take her in his arms and comfort her like he did Katie. But then, RJ didn't know that he knew she was a woman and would most likely resist. Would she resist if she knew he was on to her little secret? Probably. The woman was too stubborn for her own good.

Mason chuckled softly at the blaze that had penetrated her blue eyes when he said she wasn't leaving. He'd almost had to back away from the heat of them. RJ was most certainly one spirited filly.

RJ. What does that stand for? Ruthie Jane? Rita Jo?

Mason yawned as sleep beckoned. *Ramona J. . .*

From a distance, someone called his name. Mason fought the heaviness of sleep and forced his eyes open. The heat of the morning sun warmed his face. He raised his arms above his head, stretching the kinks from his long frame, and rammed his fist straight into the wagon wheel.

Mason winced and rubbed his knuckles as he stared up at Jimmy, who squatted beside him. "Did you hear me, Uncle Mason? I said, he's gone!"

"He? Who?" Mason lifted his hand up to his mouth and licked the thin line of blood off his knuckles.

"RJ."

four

Mason vaulted upward. A loud crack sent fingers of fire radiating pain from his forehead to the back of his head and down his neck. He bit back the urge to shout something neither Katie nor Jimmy's tender ears needed to hear. Reaching up, he pressed the injured area with the fingertips of his bruised hand.

"You okay, Uncle Mason? Your head's bleeding," Jimmy said, concern marring his boyish features. Without waiting for an answer, the boy jumped up and raced to the back of the wagon.

Mason swiped the back of his hand across his forehead. Bright red blood, warm and sticky, painted it. "This is *her* fault," he growled under his breath. He edged out from under the wagon and stood as Jimmy returned.

"Here."

Mason looked down at the fairly clean rag his nephew held in his hand.

"Much obliged, pardner. You're kind of handy to have around," he said. He put one hand on the boy's shoulder to steady himself and took the cloth. Jimmy's bright smile warmed Mason's heart. At the same time, a piercing pain gutted his insides. How could he ever say good-bye to these kids? He'd been the man in their young lives for the last several years. Jake hadn't been home in more than two years, not since Katie was a baby. He would be a stranger to her.

No matter. Jake was their father, so Jake should have his children. It all seemed very logical, but Mason's heart had a hard time agreeing. He squashed down the emotional pain and pressed the cloth to his forehead. He'd do what had to be done. The kids belonged with their father. Surely when Jake

39

found out Danielle was dead, he'd settle down and accept the responsibility of raising his own children. At least, Mason hoped he would.

After that, he would be free. Free to do whatever he wanted. Free to go wherever he wanted. Free to be alone. *Alone.* He'd never been truly alone. The thought didn't bring the comforting reassurance it had when the idea first came to him. The closer he got to finding Jake, the more he dreaded being on his own.

Mason shook his head and was instantly sorry. He pulled the cloth away and stared at the bright red stain. At the moment, he had more pressing needs. He had to find a foolish young woman riding a horse with three hooves already in its grave. Mason needed his morning coffee but decided to forgo it so he could get started looking for RJ.

His knee, injured years ago in a farming accident, hinted at a weather change. This part of the country in April was generally beautiful, but looks could be deceiving when a cold northern blast shot through and cut the temperature in half. When that happened, they could wake up with frost on the ground. Crazy woman didn't even have a cloak with her. He doubted she had any warm clothing.

"I checked on Katie. She's still sleepin'. Ya want me to start a fire for breakfast?" Jimmy asked.

"No, pard, we'll eat on the road. We've got a runaway to find."

❧

Rebekah sat in the grass alongside the trail. She wiped her eyes with the back of her hand. Prince was near death, and it was all her fault. Her faithful steed had stumbled several times during the morning ride, but she'd continued to push him. Each time he'd fallen, she'd urged him on and he'd gone. Then without warning, he fell to his knees and lay down, refusing to stand again. His sides heaved unnaturally in his effort to breathe, and Rebekah knew if he didn't get on his feet soon, he never would.

Only her quick thinking had kept her from being trapped beneath the dying horse. She hated to think what might have happened had she been wearing a dress instead of pants and not been able to jump clear. But thinking about what might have happened paled in comparison to what her faithful friend was going through right now, and she could do nothing for him. If only she had some water, maybe that would help, though Rebekah doubted anything really could. Prince had even refused the fresh prairie grass she tried to poke in the sides of his velvety mouth.

Rebekah now realized the foolishness of her hasty predawn escape. If only she'd stayed at camp, then Prince might not be fighting for his life.

Leaning forward with a hand to Prince's neck and her lips to his ear, she whispered an apology. She laid her head against his and silently berated herself for her stupidity.

"Even Mason knew you needed rest," she said softly to the horse.

Mason had slept with his head on her saddle. He must have thought that would keep her there, but it hadn't. Bareback had always been her favorite way to ride, although it was much more difficult with a carpetbag in tow. If only she could have discovered where Mason had hidden her rifle. But searching for it surely would have caused him to awaken. She'd slept deeper and longer than expected, and the birds were already singing their predawn wake-up songs as Prince first limped away from their campsite.

Now here she was, alone somewhere on the border of Arkansas and the Indian Territory, with no horse, no gun, no food, and no water.

Pulling her knees to her chest, she gave in to the tears blurring her vision. "Why is this happening, Lord? All my life Mama read the Bible to me. Even as a young child, I believed and tried to obey Your Word. What did I do wrong?"

Rebekah hiccupped and wiped her nose on her sleeve. "Aren't You going to help me?"

"Go back."

She looked around, sure she'd heard a voice. Rolling hills covered in thigh-high prairie grass dotted with clusters of trees arrayed in new green leaves were all that met her gaze.

"Go back."

Go back where?

Back home? She wasn't even sure she could find her way back to her home in southeastern Arkansas.

To Mason?

"No! I can't!" she cried out loud. *I won't.* "He doesn't want to be burdened with me."

"Go back."

Rebekah jumped to her feet. "I can't!" she screamed to the sky. "He already has his hands full. He doesn't need another mouth to feed, and I won't beg charity."

She knelt beside Prince and patted his hard jaw, her dripping tears darkening the short hairs on his neck. Huge, watery brown eyes turned her direction, and Prince blew out a weak snort. "Come on, boy. Get up. Please."

Rebekah stood and took the long leather bridle reins in both hands, pulling with all her strength, willing the big horse to rise. Prince's head slowly began to lift from the earth, but she couldn't hold the weight of him, and the reins began to slip from her grasp. Locking her knees and bracing with all her strength, Rebekah fought to hold the reins; but Prince's head fell back to the ground, and she plummeted onto her backside with an aching *thud*.

"Don't do this, Prince," she scolded the horse as she rubbed her aching rear. Rising on her knees, she crawled to her horse. "Oh Prince, please, please. . . What am I going to do without you?"

"Go back."

Rebekah raised her hands to her face in defeat. The smell of leather and horse sweat lingered on her damp palms. She clenched her jaw to kill the sob in her throat, fighting hard against the tears burning her eyes. Enough tears had been shed in the last twenty-four hours to fill a small river.

Looking up to the graying sky, Rebekah determined it to be shortly after noontime. She needed to find something to eat and drink. She didn't want to abandon Prince to suffer alone, but without her rifle, she could do nothing for him. Mason would have to tend to Prince when he came along. Turning her head, she looked to the west. Her determination faltered.

"I can't go back. Mason will be so angry. He won't want me to come back. He doesn't even like me. I'm a burden he doesn't need."

She rose to her feet. With resolve, Rebekah picked up her carpetbag and walked west into the chilly breeze, hoping and praying she'd find water over the next hill.

Several hills later, Rebekah began to wonder why she'd felt such an urge to get away from Mason. Sure, he'd snapped at her and been upset, but wasn't it because of her stubborn insistence to do things herself when she was far too weak? Her steps slowed. The boots, an ancient pair of Curtis's that were several sizes too large for her, rubbed painful blisters on the sides of her feet.

Rebekah limped over to a grove of trees just off the trail. She dropped her carpetbag and leaned against a tall oak, relishing the support it offered her weary body. A sudden blast of cold air from the northwest taunted the tree's juvenile leaves, while streams of dark, ominous clouds drifted across the gray sky. Wrapping her arms around her chest, Rebekah slid down the trunk of the tree, huddling in a ball, her mind transporting her back to happier, warmer days.

As Rebekah nestled in a quilt with Davy on her lap, sitting in front of the fireplace, they'd listened to their mother read God's Word. One of her mother's favorite verses filtered through her cloud of confusion: *"For I know the thoughts that I think toward you, saith the Lord, thoughts of peace, and not of evil, to give you an expected end."*

Rebekah sucked in a shaky breath. Surely this wasn't the

end for her. God's expected end? Surely not. Why would He bring her out in the middle of nowhere just to die? When her mother had read the verse back home, it had always instilled hope in Rebekah. Hope for a home of her own with a husband who loved her and children to cuddle and nurture. As Rebekah reached her teen years, her mother had often said, "Sooner or later, some handsome man will come along and sweep you off your feet."

"Sooner or later," Rebekah murmured. Not if this was her expected end.

"Thoughts of peace, and not of evil. . ." That's the key. Peace. Warmth spread through Rebekah's being as she realized the truth. Thoughts of this being her expected end did not bring her peace; thus they must not be from God. Dying on the prairie was not her expected end. She knew it all the way to her tiptoes.

"Go back."

She heard the words in her mind once more. With sudden composure and deliberate resolve, she jumped to her feet. She picked up her bag, raised her chin, and turned back toward the east.

"All right, Mason Whoever-You-Are, here I come."

The abrupt *ping* of a rifle shot halted the words in her mouth. Her head jerked up. She squinted her eyes, staring off into the distance. Another rapid blast rang out, echoing across the hills. Rebekah began to shake. Fearful images of merciless armed men filled her mind. Her newfound peace and confidence quickly evaporated as icy fear twisted around her heart.

"Oh, Lord, I'm sorry. Sorry for my stubbornness. Sorry for my independence. Forgive me for not being grateful when you sent Mason to help me."

The tears she had successfully held at bay the past half hour spilled forth in a torrent. The tight knot within her begged for release as she turned around again and raced behind the huge oak tree. Once again, she slid to the ground.

"Please, God, show me a way out of this awful mess."

❧

Mason rubbed his jaw, which was starting to ache from being clenched all morning. He needed a shave. His bristly beard had grown out the past few days since he'd been rationing their remaining water. As soon as it rained or they came upon a creek, he would shave it off. *RJ must think I look like a hillbilly.*

RJ had headed west; he was sure of it. Shortly past their campsite, he'd happened upon a fresh pile of manure. Since he'd seen no other horses, Mason felt certain it belonged to Prince.

As far as he could tell, the crazy woman had taken nothing with her except a small carpetbag. She even had the gumption to ride off bareback since he'd used her saddle for a not-so-soft pillow. Not for the first time, Mason wished he had a faster horse. On a good horse, he could cover in a half hour the ground that it had taken the slower-moving draft horses all morning to cover. They were great for pulling the heavy Conestoga wagon, but he had to have patience, something he was running very low on at the moment. Besides, even if he had a quick horse, he couldn't ride off and leave Katie and Jimmy alone. That was the whole reason he had sold his other horses before making the move west.

"Look!" Jimmy reached for Mason's sleeve and grabbed a piece of his arm along with it. The sharp pain reminded him he should have been keeping his mind on the job at hand.

"Isn't that RJ's horse?"

Mason squinted and pulled his hat down on his forehead to block the early afternoon sun as he followed Jimmy's finger. He grimaced when his hat pressed against the cut on his head. His heart lodged in his throat when he saw RJ's horse lying alongside the trail, a ring of buzzards eagerly awaiting its certain death. He stood and scanned the countryside, clear to the horizon, but he couldn't see RJ anywhere. A band of tension tightened around his chest, threatening to choke his breathing. Why had he been so crotchety with her? Maybe if he'd been more hospitable, she wouldn't have run off.

"Whoa," he crooned to the big horses as he pulled the equine quartet to a stop. Setting the brake, he grabbed his rifle and fired into the air, scattering squawking buzzards in different directions. In one big leap, he lunged over the side of the wagon and approached the horse. It only took Mason a moment to determine Prince had been down too long and wouldn't be able to rise again. He didn't like what he had to do, but the animal needed to be put out of its misery. The whites of the horse's eyes and his flaring nostrils showed his frantic fear of the buzzards.

"Jimmy, get in the back of the wagon with Katie," Mason ordered.

Jimmy opened his mouth to object then seemed to realize what Mason was preparing to do. He gave a quick nod and hopped over the seat.

Mason cocked his rifle and skillfully shot the horse in the head, putting it out of its misery. Slowly he walked around the large body, studying the footprints in the dirt and the places where the prairie grass was smashed down. As best he could tell, RJ hadn't been injured when the horse most likely collapsed.

Why hadn't she listened when he warned her about the danger of riding her horse in its condition? Especially when they didn't have enough water available to give him a decent drink. Mason grimaced. If they didn't happen upon water soon, he'd be shooting his own horses.

West. Even being on foot, the crazy woman walked west instead of coming back to him. Didn't she have any sense at all? What if she'd run into outlaws or Indians? The muscle clenched in his aching jaw. Had he not hidden her rifle in hopes of keeping her from leaving, she'd be armed right now. If anything happened to her, he'd be as much to blame as she.

Mason climbed back in the wagon and released the brake. "He-yah!" he yelled, startling the big horses into a lumbering trot. "Jimmy, get up here and keep a close eye out for RJ," he ordered.

"Unca Mathon, I gots ta go," Katie called from the back of the wagon.

"Not now, Katie. You're gonna have to wait. I have to find RJ." Mason didn't look back. If he saw his niece's pouting lips and big blue eyes, he might waver. He had to find RJ before some wild creature or ruffian did. As they crested the next hill, Mason pulled the horses to a stop and stood, once again scanning the area.

"See anything, pard?"

Jimmy shook his head. "Why ya think he left in the middle of the night?"

Stubbornness and independence, he nearly blurted out loud. But he wouldn't mention those character traits to a child. Mason clicked the horses forward. "Probably just too proud to accept help. Some folks feel the need to do things for themselves."

"Kinda sounds like you."

He gave Jimmy a sideways glance of disbelief. "Am I that bad?"

Jimmy's cheeks turned a shade of rosy pink, almost matching his sunburned nose. "Well," he started, as if unsure of continuing, "you do like to boss everyone around."

"I *am* the boss." He eyed Jimmy, unsure what point he was trying to make.

"Yeah, but. . .sometimes you boss grown-ups, too. Pa used to say that." Jimmy ducked his head and picked at the edge of his frayed shirt.

Mason's mind raced. Jake said he was bossy? He struggled to think back two years to when Jake had been around. As if he'd been doused with a bucket of frigid water, he shivered as some of Jake's last words rocked his mind. *"Danielle don't need me around when she's got you. A woman's s'posed to look to her husband for things, not her brother. You two's closer than a possum and its young'uns."*

Ducking his head, Mason stared at the dirt on his boots. His father had always told him he was too stubborn for his own good. But being stubborn helped him survive all those harsh whippings his father had given him—even when his mother begged the colonel to stop. Mason grimaced. His father was stubborn, too. Was he becoming the very man he despised?

"Look! What's that over there behind that tree?" Jimmy cried.

five

Glancing in the direction Jimmy pointed, Mason's gaze raked the area, searching for some sign of RJ. In the distance, a hint of soft blue against the green tangle of honeysuckle bushes and wind-tossed grasses snagged his attention.

RJ.

Something deep within him wanted to shout out thanks to God, but he stuffed it down. He wasn't on speaking terms with God these days.

Giving the reins a strong flick, he turned his horses toward her, wishing their plodding feet could move faster. Impatience won out. He jerked back the reins, and the big horses lumbered to a walk. Standing to his feet, he was ready to jump out of the wagon the moment it shuddered to a stop. Mason yanked the brake back and threw the reins to Jimmy.

"Stay put," he told the boy. Grabbing his rifle, he jumped down and set off in a dead run toward his target, certain the blue he'd seen was RJ's shirt.

"RJ!" Jimmy yelled. Fear laced the young voice that was nearly drowned out by the cold wind.

RJ lay on the ground, unmoving. Mason lengthened his steps, dodging prairie-dog holes and leaping over a downed tree. Maybe it was urgency he felt, or fear, or guilt for his harsh treatment of the girl; but his legs, usually agile and swift, felt weighted and sluggish.

"RJ," he called, closing the distance to her prone body. He willed her to move, to let him know she'd heard his calls, but her body remained motionless. Mason's heart plummeted, fearing the worse. He kicked his stride up a notch, his boots thudding against the hard ground. Caught by the breeze, his hat flew off, leaving his sweating head exposed to the chilling elements. He ignored it—ignored the plummeting temperatures and the brisk winds fingering his neck and slipping into his shirt. Easing down beside her, he set his rifle aside.

"RJ. It's Mason."

He checked her arms and head, looking for cuts and bruises, but saw no signs of injury. Still worried she might have wounds he couldn't see, he eased her shoulders off the ground, cradling her in his lap. Without the old brown felt hat covering RJ's features, Mason was gifted with his first real look at the girl in the sunlight. He took a moment to catch his breath and gather his senses while he studied her pale face.

Like tiny feathers dancing in the breeze, long strands of saddle brown hair swirled around her chilled cheeks. A smattering of cinnamon-colored freckles dotted her pink, turned-up nose. Long black lashes rested in a half-moon against sunburned cheeks, hiding her sky blue eyes. He wanted to see those blue eyes snapping in defiance again, but RJ didn't seem to realize he was even there.

"RJ." He whispered her name as he caressed her brow. "Come on, sugar, wake up," he said with a little more force. Then he shook her softly and willed her eyes to open. He nearly yelled for joy when she moved.

"Mmm, cold," RJ murmured against his shirt. Her body shivered and Mason lifted her closer, pulling her against his chest. Turning his body so that the brisk wind buffeted his back, he shielded her from nature's assault. Hugging her and rubbing her arms and back to generate heat, he listened to her soft moans and battled his own private storm.

❧

Snuggled in her quilt, safe at home in bed, Rebekah felt warmth filling her being. The soft, comforting voice poured over her like warm honey on fresh-baked bread. She leaned into the voice rumbling against her cheek and relished its calming reassurance.

"Suguh, wake up," it called again.

Rebekah rubbed her eyes, realizing it was already dawn. Her heart skipped a beat. If she didn't get up soon, Pa would climb the ladder to her small loft and take a switch to her. She had to rise, but she didn't want to leave her cocoon of warmth.

"RJ, you've gotta wake up." The voice was firm this time, the gentle crooning gone.

Forcing one abnormally heavy eyelid open, Rebekah peeked out at a blurry shirt pocket with a torn flap. The faint scent of campfire smoke lingered within its threads. Mason's shirt. She blinked twice, her gaze clearing, but it was still there. With her palm, she pushed against Mason's chest. His arms yielded, allowing her to lean back and look into his concerned face.

Instant relief flooded her. *Oh, thank You, Lord!*

Suddenly the reality of her hasty predawn decision hit her.

"I—I killed Prince." She hiccupped back a sob.

Mason pulled her back into his arms, tucking her head under his chin. "No, sugar, that horse was ancient. He probably would've died soon even if you hadn't ridden off on him," he said softly, smoothing her hair with his big hand.

She wanted to linger in the warmth of his embrace. Her problems seemed so far away with his strong arms and gentle voice comforting her. But the problems weren't going away—and one of the problems was Mason. With a start, she realized the glare that had been in his eyes ever since they'd met was gone.

She sighed and pushed away from Mason's chest again.

"Can you stand up?" he asked.

Nodding, she pressed against the ground and struggled to her feet, the chilly wind making a valiant effort to knock her down again. Mason hopped up and reached out to steady her. When her legs trembled, threatening to dump her on the ground, Rebekah took hold of Mason's arm.

A movement caught her eye, and she turned her head just as the stiff breeze picked up her hat and sent it sailing away.

Rebekah froze. The only part of her body moving was her long braid, flapping against her back.

He knows!

Swallowing back the sudden queasiness rising to her throat, Rebekah took a deep breath and looked up. Amusement flickered in the gaze that met hers. Mason's inviting mouth quirked up at one corner, along with his dark eyebrows.

Rebekah licked her lips with the tip of her dry tongue. "That's why you let me sleep with Katie, isn't it? You knew I was a woman."

Mason gave her a single quick nod. "Didn't figure you'd want to sleep under the wagon with me." His mouth twitched in his obvious effort to hold back a grin.

Rebekah straightened, not particularly enjoying the pleasure he derived from her discomfort. She wanted desperately to remove her hands from his arm, but she didn't trust her legs, weakened again by a day without food. "How long have you known?" She narrowed her eyes at him.

"Ever since I found you sprawled out along the trail. Your hat was off and I saw your braid."

She couldn't resist smacking him in the chest and nearly laughed herself when his amused expression turned to surprise. "Why didn't you say anything?"

He looked down at his boots then caught her gaze. "I figured you had your reasons. That you probably didn't feel safe enough around me to come clean." Mason looked toward the wagon, and Rebekah noticed a flicker in his jaw.

She felt grateful for his honesty. Her cheeks warmed when she realized how secure she'd felt in his arms. When he wasn't growling at her like an old bear, Mason was rather pleasant to be around. Maybe she had misjudged him. Just maybe, traveling with Mason wouldn't be as bad as she'd first thought.

Rebekah didn't want the flare of anger to be rekindled in his eyes, but she had to know. "Are you angry with me?"

His head jerked back in her direction, and she noticed a

fresh cut on his forehead. He stood with his hands on his hips, eyes hooded, lips pursed into a solid line.

Uh-oh, he's mad. Praying her legs wouldn't betray her, Rebekah took a step back and crossed her arms over her chest.

"I ought to be. That was a stupid, dangerous thing you did, taking off without food, rifle, and especially water. What were you thinking—no, wait, you weren't thinking, were you? You scared ten years off my life."

Rebekah ventured a peek at Mason's face.

"I ought to be mad, but I'm just so thankful you aren't dead. . . ."

A smile broke its way through her mask of uncertainty. *He's not mad at me.* Her mother's words flittered across her mind. *"Sooner or later, you'll meet a handsome man who will sweep you off your feet."* Rebekah didn't think she'd mind too much if Mason was that man.

"There's just one thing I gotta know."

"What's that?" she asked, squelching back the ridiculous notion of her and Mason ever getting together. *He doesn't even like me.*

Mason combed his fingers through his long dark hair. Rebekah wondered if his red ears were a result of the freezing wind or something else. Butterflies danced in her tummy when Mason's mouth turned up in an embarrassed grin.

"What does RJ stand for? I swear I was awake half the night trying to figure that out."

&

"Uh. . .RJ's your initials, not something you made up, right?"

The sweet smile that had been on RJ's face faded, and a spark ignited in her eyes. "You're not accusing me of lying, are you? Why would I make that up?" She tugged her arms tighter against her chest, whether in frustration or to ward off the cold, Mason wasn't sure.

He cleared his throat. "Well, you *are* the one wearing a disguise." He smiled back, daring her to disagree.

"I never lied to you. My name is Rebekah Jane Bailey, though most people call me Rebekah." She thrust her chin in the air then wobbled in the breeze, as if she hadn't the strength to withstand it.

"Well, Rebekah Jane Bailey...uh, Rebekah, I'm Mason Danfield, and we'd best be getting back to the wagon fore you freeze your pretty little self to death."

She nodded and stuck her hand out to him. "Pleasure to meet you, Mr. Danfield."

One eyebrow and the corner of his mouth tilted up in mock consternation. "Mr. Danfield," he said with added precise emphasis, "is my daddy, and he's back in Georgia, living on his plantation. I'm Mason." As if to prove he was in no mood to argue, he took the hand she held out and put it on his shoulder. When her eyebrows pinched into a questioning V, he bent down and lifted her up. He pulled her against his chest, smiling at her stunned expression.

Rebekah squirmed, kicking her feet and pushing against him. "I can walk. I don't need you to carry me."

"It's warmer this way." He took a few steps, stooped down, and holding Rebekah up with his knee, picked up her carpetbag. Turning, he shuffled over to a nearby bush. "Grab your hat." He bent down and she reached out, pulling against his shoulder, and grabbed her hat, which clung to a honeysuckle vine. Then she cuddled against his chest.

Mason started for the wagon, his thoughts on the young woman in his arms. Rebekah was shorter and lighter weight than Annie had been. Annie's Swedish heritage had been evident in her white blond hair and tall, sturdy frame. Mason glanced down at Rebekah's thick braid lying over her shoulder and across her chest. He'd always tried to get Annie to grow out her shoulder-length hair, but she'd refused, saying long hair took too much work.

Mason drew in a ragged breath. Why was he comparing the two women? He wasn't looking to replace Annie. She was the love of his life. Mason stopped at the back of the wagon and helped Rebekah crawl inside.

"You're a girl!" Jimmy stood in the middle of the wagon with his hands on his hips, looking at RJ as if he'd been betrayed. Mason understood how the boy felt. RJ—no, Rebekah—had many secrets, but thankfully she hadn't lied to him. His nephew barreled toward the tailgate, slithered over the side, and dropped to the ground. Jimmy gazed up at him accusingly. "Did you know?"

Mason nodded.

"Why didn't you say something? A man shares his secrets with another man that he wouldn't tell no girl."

Tightening his lips, Mason struggled to hold in his chuckle, wondering what *manly* secrets Jimmy might've shared with Rebekah. "I figured she had her reasons for keeping her identity a secret, and she'd tell us when she trusted us."

Jimmy shook his head and stomped off, mumbling.

Katie hopped up, leaning out of the back of the wagon and reaching out to him. "RJ's a girwl! Yippee! I'm glad." Her bright smile ignited a warmth in his chest that swept through his whole body. "Unca Mathon, I still gots ta go."

He chuckled and reached for his niece.

"It's cold!" Katie burrowed into his chest as he lifted her out of the wagon. "Is it gonna snow?"

"No, sugar, it's too late in the spring for snow. It'll just be cold for a bit, and then it'll warm up again."

Mason set Katie down in the grass and ambled over to where his hat rested, pressed against a mammoth oak tree. The tree branches groaned their resistance to the stiff breeze, and the young leaves hung on for dear life, twisting one way and then the other. He smacked his hat against his leg then pressed it on his head as he gazed heavenward, watching the dark gray clouds drifting past with the speed of an agile roadrunner. He glanced back at his four draft horses. A pang of pity shot through him as he stared at their hanging heads. They needed water, and if they didn't get it soon, he'd have to shoot them. With two small children and a willful young woman, it would be a long walk to the middle of Indian Territory where Jake was supposed to be.

He looked heavenward again.

Come on, we need some rain.

The words were the closest thing to a prayer that he'd uttered in the past six months.

six

Sometime in the middle of the night the rains came, fast and furious. A sudden blast of thunder and the initial *pitter-patter* of raindrops alerted Mason to the pending downpour. With the earthy scent of parched dirt and fresh rain filling his nostrils, he scooped up Jimmy and their bedding and made a dash for the protection of the wagon.

The hasty movement didn't faze Jimmy from his deep sleep. With his arms full, Mason stood just inside the tailgate, allowing time for his eyes to adjust to the darkness. A bolt of lightning flashed, illuminating the wagon's insides, and Mason eased Jimmy down along the side next to Katie. A smile tilted his lips when he saw Rebekah, sleeping with her arm around his niece.

After adjusting his bedding at the foot of the wagon, Mason eased down. He'd have to sleep sitting up in order to give Rebekah plenty of room so as not to encroach the rules of propriety. He knew he shouldn't even be in the wagon with her asleep, but he couldn't afford to get drenched in this cold and take sick. If he were down, that would leave the other three helplessly on their own.

Under the safety of the canopy, Mason listened to the steady downpour. Relief flooded him. He was thankful he'd left the lids off the two large water barrels attached to the side of the wagon. He had hoped it would rain; now he hoped the rain wouldn't continue too long and turn the trail into a mud-soaked river. Thunder boomed and another flash of lightning brightened the wagon. Rebekah bolted upright, blinking the sleep from her eyes. Even in the dark, he could tell she stared wide-eyed at him.

"W—what are you doing in here?" She pulled her quilt over

her chest, not that it mattered since she still wore her clothes.

"In case you didn't notice, it's pouring outside."

"Oh?"

"Looks like we're gonna get a real toad strangler. I didn't want Jimmy and me to get soaked and possibly sick. 'Sides, I have to keep an eye on the canopy when it rains." The sky lit up, and Mason motioned toward the top of the wagon. "If the top puddles, it'll start leaking and drench everything inside. This is an old wagon, and the canvas has some sun rot. I couldn't see the point in investing a lot of money in a new one when we only needed it for about a month. It's not all that far from St. Louis to the Indian Territory."

He knew he was babbling; he just didn't know why. Running off at the mouth wasn't one of his normal characteristics.

"It's okay," Rebekah whispered. "I really hate storms. I'm glad you're here."

Lightning exploded in the night sky so close he could smell the burn. For a moment, it seemed as if someone had lit the lantern hanging from the wagon's ribbings. Mason watched Rebekah pull her quilt clear up to her chin as if to protect herself from the storm—or from him. Her wide eyes looked childlike. Long, sleep-tossed, unbraided hair wrapped around her like a cloak, and Mason had a deep urge to bury his hands in her unkempt tendrils.

Roaring thunder shook the wagon, and in the next instant Rebekah dropped her quilt and scrambled to his side, cowering against his arm. Mason reached for the quilt, tucked it around her, then wrapped his arm around her shoulders, pulling her against his chest. Though surprised by Rebekah's reaction to the storm, he relished the warmth her nearness brought. Outside, he and Jimmy had snuggled together under their quilts, but the frosty temperature had chilled him to the bone.

"I–I'm sorry to be such a baby and so much trouble. I promise tomorrow I'll start pulling my own weight," Rebekah whispered against his shirt, the heat of her breath warming a spot on his chest.

"Shhh. Don't worry about it." Wisps of her hair tickled his chin. With a deep sigh, he brushed it down, stroking her long mane. "I don't care much for storms either, though I'm thankful for the rain. I was getting worried."

"What about?"

"We're running short on water. I was concerned I might have to put the horses down."

Rebekah pushed away from his chest. He could feel her staring at him through the dark. "You wouldn't do that, would you?"

"I shot Prince."

Rebekah gasped and Mason grimaced. "Rebekah," he whispered, "Prince was dying. He was suffering."

"I know and it's all my fault."

Mason heard her suck back a sob. He straightened and leaned forward. In the dark, he reached for Rebekah's face. Lightning flashed. In that brief moment, he smoothed her hair from her face and laid his palms against her cheeks. He wished he could see her eyes, but it was dark again. "Listen to me, Rebekah. Prince was an old horse. It was simply his time. I don't want to hear any more about your killing him. Do you understand?"

He felt her nod. Once again, thunder jolted the wagon. A horse whinnied somewhere outside. Mason pulled Rebekah against his side and wrapped his arm around her shivering shoulders. It was warmer for both of them that way, he told himself.

She wrapped one arm around his back and rested her head against his shoulder. Her warm breath tickled his chin, and her long hair covered his left arm. She smelled of campfire smoke and flowers. She weighed next to nothing—it was almost like holding Katie. No, Rebekah was much different from Katie.

He could tell Rebekah liked to be held and cuddled. Annie hadn't cared for either. She'd been affectionate, but she always said she couldn't go to sleep if he held her, so after a brief hug and kiss good night, she'd skedaddled over to her side of the bed.

Mason enjoyed holding Rebekah. As a boy, he'd hugged his mother a lot. Of course, hugging Rebekah was much different than hugging his mother. After his mother's death, the only hugs he'd received had been his sister Danielle's, at least until Annie had come along. His father's stoic personality had kept the man from showing any sort of affection. Mason was thankful he took after his mother in that respect. If he ever married again, he'd make sure to choose an affectionate woman.

"Mason, can I ask you a question?" Rebekah whispered against his cheek.

"Sure."

"How old are you?"

Mason pushed against a supply crate with his foot and shifted to a better position. "I'm twenty-six. How about you?"

"Twenty-one."

Twenty-one? Mason blinked against the darkness. He'd thought for sure she wasn't a day over seventeen.

"Have you—I mean—you're not—married, are you?" Rebekah stiffened in his arms.

Mason's stomach clenched. He hadn't spoken to anyone about Annie or her death since the funeral. Neighbors had brought food for the three of them, but he'd refused to talk about the sudden deaths. He couldn't. Could he now? Now that six months had passed?

Rebekah pushed against his chest with her palm, tying to ease out of his embrace. Thunder boomed, and she stiffened but didn't cower in fear this time. "Um. . .never mind. I don't mean to be prying. I just thought since we can't sleep and we'll be traveling together, it would be nice to know each other better." She squirmed again. "And, Mason, let me go."

Mason tightened his arms, not allowing her to escape. He knew he shouldn't, but he wanted to hold her—needed to hold her—if he was going to tell her about Annie. "Shhh.

Just relax. The storm's not over yet." He pulled her head to his shoulder, gently pinning it there with his palm, thankful she didn't resist. As if they had a mind of their own, his fingers buried themselves in her wealth of hair.

❧

Rebekah felt Mason tremble—or was it her? She'd never been in a man's arms before. As far back as she could remember, Curtis had never hugged her. Mason's solid torso felt so different than being hugged by her mother's soft body. As much as Rebekah enjoyed the security of being in his arms, she felt she should move away, but now she couldn't. Her head was anchored against Mason's shoulder by his strong hand; his short beard tickled her forehead. He took a deep, shuddering breath, and Rebekah couldn't resist laying her free arm across his chest.

"I was married. . .for nearly two years." He paused, and Rebekah wondered if she should ask what happened.

"Annie died." Mason exhaled a deep sigh as if it required a huge effort to broach the subject. "She was carrying our first child. My sister, Danielle, Jimmy and Katie's mother, was with her. They both died when the wagon they were riding in overturned as they were crossing a river in a sudden storm. The water in the river was usually only a few inches deep, but not that afternoon. They got caught in a flash flood."

Ah. That explained his desire to hold her. Maybe the storm disturbed him as much as it did her. She wrapped her arm farther around his chest, and he laid his head against hers. Maybe her holding him would help comfort him. *How awful to lose so much in one day.*

"I'm so sorry, Mason."

Here in the dark, in Mason's arms, he didn't seem so intimidating. He was warm, secure, needy. She felt safe in a man's arms for the first time in her life. He, too, had suffered and endured the horrible pain of losing someone he loved.

"I don't know if the pain of that day will ever go away," he whispered against her hair.

"Time has a way of lessening the pain. And God can help the most."

Mason suddenly stiffened. "God doesn't care about our suffering. And what do you know of such pain? Surely at just twenty-one, you haven't been married before." His voice carried a harshness that hadn't been there before.

Releasing her hold on Mason, she pulled her arm down against her chest. *He's mad at God.* Of that much she was certain.

"I know the pain of losing someone you love more than life."

"Who, Rebekah? Who did you lose?" His voice softened to that slow Southern drawl she loved to listen to.

"M—my mother and my little brother, Davy. They died last year from influenza. I tried so hard to save them." She choked back a sob. "Pa. . .uh, Curtis, was out on a hunting trip, and I was afraid to leave them to go for the doctor. He was so angry with me when he got back home. Said it was my fault." Tears wet her cheeks, and she turned her face into the warmth of Mason's shirt. His arms tightened around her.

"He hurried for the doctor, but Davy was already gone by the time he got back, and Ma was close to death. If I'd left them alone and gone for the doctor, they might still be alive." The familiar pain tore at her breast. How many times had she played the "what-if" game? Her fingers tightened on Mason's shirt.

"Shhh, sugar, don't cry. We'll get through this together." Mason said the words against her forehead. He called her "suguh" with that smooth voice of his. Chills, from something other than the cold damp air, raced down her spine. He gently kissed her temple, loosing a storm within her unlike any she'd ever known. She wanted to feel his kiss upon her lips. Just once.

She sniffed back her tears and tilted her head. His gentle kisses angled past her ear and down her jawline. Rebekah's heart pounded louder than the thunder booming in the distance. Their lips connected like a whisper. The warm touch of his mouth deepened on hers, sending a shock wave through her entire body. It was a kiss her tired soul could melt into—her first kiss.

Suddenly Mason stiffened and pulled away. "Rebekah? Uh. . .that was a mistake."

Rebekah's emotions whirled like a leaf in an eddy of wind and then skidded to a halt. She jerked from his embrace, her lips still warm and moist from his kiss. Instantly the chill in the wagon battered her as hard as his words. Grabbing her quilt, she crawled back to her sleeping spot and lay down.

The kiss left her weak and confused. She was stunned at her own eager response to Mason's kiss, but she was more shocked by his words. *"That was a mistake."*

No, Mason, it was the best thing I've ever experienced.

"Rebekah? I don't know what came over me." She heard his voice edging closer.

"Just leave me alone." She spat out the words.

"Fine! That's just fine with me."

She heard Mason's shuffling as he exited the wagon, and she shuddered at the cold breeze that followed. The worst of the storm had blown past them. Rebekah listened to the gentle patter of the raindrops against the wagon's covering. Jimmy's and Katie's steady breathing filled the air. Peace reigned everywhere except within her.

Lord, was it a mistake to enjoy Mason's kiss? You know he's the only man I've ever kissed. Does kissing a man always feel like that? Like an explosion? As if a fire were being lit in my belly? How could something that felt so good be a mistake? I don't understand.

Warm tears trailed down her cheeks. *I was a fool to think Mason had a speck of niceness in him. He probably hugged me just so he could get warm.*

"But he called me 'suguh,'" she whispered out loud. Rebekah turned on her side as the tears continued to fall. She didn't want to lose her heart to this bear of a man who despised her, but she feared he'd already staked a claim on a quarter section.

She took a deep, trembling breath and resolved he wouldn't claim any more. Until she could find a way to get to Denver, Rebekah determined to keep her distance and make sure she did her fair share of the work. She wouldn't give him cause to lower his opinion of her any further.

Her tears slowed as her determination deepened. Finally, sleepiness claimed her body with its soothing, relaxing heaviness. Rebekah felt herself drifting toward that land without thoughts and pain. A place without those black eyes burning their way into her heart.

A sudden icy coldness splattering against her cheek pulled her back from her haven of rest. With her sleeve, she wiped it away. Instantly the frigid moistness returned, bringing a friend with it. *Drip! Plop!*

"Nooo." *The roof!*

seven

For the past two days, Mason's level of conversation with Rebekah had been reduced to a series of grunts and nods. He was so angry with himself for kissing her. One minute he was spilling his grief about Annie, and the next he was kissing Rebekah.

Mason shook the sweet memory from his mind. How could Rebekah stir up such feelings within him when they'd just met? He didn't like it. It felt like a betrayal of Annie's memory. He wouldn't let it happen again.

Jerking his hat from his head, he smacked it against his pant leg, sending dust flying. Rebekah looked up from the campfire where she was stirring a pot of rabbit stew. The tantalizing odor caused his stomach to rumble nearly as loudly as the thunderstorm had roared the other night. At least one good thing had happened. Once Jimmy discovered how good a cook Rebecca was, his anger at her being a female shriveled up like a piece of bacon in a hot skillet.

Two days ago, they'd huddled together to get warm. Now spring had returned, bringing a taste of summer with it. How could the weather change so fast here? Mason ran his fingers through his sweaty hair. Weather in the heart of the nation was unpredictable—challenging.

"We're done." Jimmy smiled up at him.

"Both barrels are full?" Mason asked, setting his sweat-stained hat on a rock to dry.

Jimmy glanced sideways at Katie and scowled. "Yeah, but it weren't easy. Katie got more water on her than in the barrels."

"Nuh-uh," Katie said. "I helped lots. Jimmy spwashed me."

Mason smiled at Katie. The braids Rebekah had so meticulously woven together that morning were frayed and dripping.

Water dribbled from Katie's undergarments, which were stained dark by her numerous encounters with the mud along the creek bank. Rebekah showed good sense in removing Katie's dress before allowing her to help Jimmy.

"Guess she'll be needing a bath after lunch," Rebekah commented.

"Nuh-uh, I gived me one." Katie smiled and smoothed her filthy chemise.

Mason laughed out loud, and with joyous moments in short supply, it felt good. "Oh, sugar." He scooped her up in his arms and smacked a kiss on her moist cheek. "I think it'd do us all good to take a bath. It's been way too long."

"Not me. I ain't takin' no bath." Jimmy crossed his arms and jutted his chin in the air.

Setting Katie on the ground, Mason straightened and turned a stern but playful gaze toward Jimmy. "Oh, yeah?"

"Yeah." Jimmy glanced from Mason to Rebekah and back, as if searching for an ally.

"I don't know, Rebekah." Mason turned to look at her. "What do you think?" She set the wooden spoon on a rock and rested her hands on her hips. "Think this boy needs a bath?"

Rebekah blinked as if surprised by his teasing; then she gave him a conspiratorial grin followed by a playful wink. Mason's heart did a little flip. "Oh, I don't know," she said. "I think the question is more *when* he needs a bath than *if* he needs one."

It was the most she'd spoken to him in days. Pleased that she sided with him so readily in spite of the chasm of unspoken words separating them, Mason smiled.

Jimmy scowled at her.

"You know, I think you're right." Mason took a step toward the boy. "In fact, I think we'd all enjoy lunch a bit more if he bathed beforehand."

Jimmy's dark eyes widened. "What's that supposed to mean?"

"Rebekah, you think Jimmy's got time for a bath before lunch?" He wiggled his eyebrows up and down, hoping she'd continue the playful banter.

She picked up a cast-iron lid from a nearby rock and set it on top of the kettle of stew. Her lips curved into an amused grin. "I don't think it would hurt this stew to cook a bit longer."

"Well, then, I guess now's as good a time as any." Mason turned toward Jimmy.

"You mean, right now?" Jimmy asked, his voice laced with disbelief and his eyes almost ready to pop out of their sockets. "But I don't want no bath, Uncle Mason."

From behind him, Mason heard Katie's excited giggle. "I wanna help. I wants ta spwash him."

Mason edged toward Jimmy. "Aw, come on, pardner, it's not that bad. Just think, you'll get to cool off and clean up all at once."

"I'll get him some clean clothes to put on," Rebekah offered as she moved behind Jimmy and toward the wagon.

"I don't want no stinkin' bath!" Jimmy yelled. He backed away from Mason, casting cautious glances toward the water.

Mason chuckled from deep within. "You're the one who's stinkin', son."

Jimmy tilted his chin down and sniffed his shirt. "I don't smell no worse than you."

An unladylike snort erupted from Rebekah as her shoulders curled and she bent forward. Her eyes danced with amusement as she struggled to hold back her tight-lipped smile. She sucked in her lips and raised her eyebrows as if daring him to object to Jimmy's observation.

With one eyebrow raised, Mason looked at her in mock indignation. He rather enjoyed this playful side of Rebekah.

"Well, Jimmy does have a point," she finally said, still struggling for some semblance of control. "I—" She seemed to struggle to speak. "I'm just glad I'm upwind of the two of you."

Mason stopped in midstep. "I'm not taking a bath in the middle of the day."

One of Rebekah's eyebrows and one side of her mouth tilted upward. "Hypocrite."

"This isn't about me. It's about Jimmy." Mason straightened. "C'mon, Jimmy, grab the soap and let's get you washed up."

"Me, too. I wants ta be washed up." Katie ran over and grabbed Rebekah by the leg. "I want Webekah to wash me up."

A roguish grin tilted Mason's lips. "You know, Katie, now that you mention it, Rebekah doesn't exactly smell too good herself."

All amusement faded from Rebekah's face, and Mason had to hold back his own chuckle. A rosy tinge painted her cheeks. Somehow he didn't think it was from working over a hot fire on such a warm, humid day. With her palm, she gently fingered Katie's hair. It suddenly dawned on him how much Katie had taken to Rebekah. His stomach clenched and he felt his smile fade. He didn't want Katie to have to suffer another loss when Rebekah left.

"I—I don't have any clean clothes to wear," Rebekah said. She stood rigidly and thrust her chin in the air.

Mason read the unspoken words he knew must be on the tip of her tongue. *I'm not about to wash when you're anywhere nearby.*

An idea popped into his mind. "I know just what you need." He turned and hurried toward the wagon and climbed in. After rummaging through a trunk of clothing, he found his objective.

Hopping down off the tailgate and sending dust flying, he turned and marched toward Rebekah, smiling inwardly, knowing he'd won this round. He relished her questioning stare.

"Close your eyes."

Rebekah's curious gaze caught his. Excitement filled him, knowing she'd be pleased with his gift.

"Go on, Rebekah, close your eyes," he encouraged. *C'mon, trust me.*

"What you got, Unca Mathon?" Katie giggled. "You gots a th'pwise for Webekah?"

Mason nodded at Katie then looked back at Rebekah. A

tiny smile graced her lips, sending his stomach bucking like a back-busting bronc. Rebekah's eyelids eased shut.

From behind his back, Mason pulled out a dark green cotton dress and gave it a gentle shake. Holding it under his chin, he smoothed the wrinkles and then held it up by the shoulders.

"Ohhh," Katie exclaimed. "That's Mommy's."

Obviously overcome by curiosity, Rebekah peeked out of one eye. She threw him a questioning look; then her eyes twinkled with what looked like delight. Mason felt a surge of pride race through him. Suddenly Rebekah's pleasant expression was replaced by something else as she turned toward Katie.

"That's your mama's dress?"

"Uh-huh." Katie nodded.

Rebekah knelt down and took Katie's hand, turning the little girl toward her. "It must be a special dress if it was your mama's. I understand if you don't want me to wear it. I have a dress in my bag I can wear, but I need to wash it first."

"You can wear it," Katie offered with a hesitant smile.

Rebekah glanced up at Mason. A warmth flooded him at her concern for Katie's feelings. He felt his wall of reserve toward Rebekah crumbling, and he didn't know what to do about it.

"Are you sure, sweetie? You really don't mind if I borrow your mama's dress?"

Katie nodded and Rebekah looked toward Jimmy.

"What about you, Jimmy? Would you mind if I borrowed your mama's dress? I promise to give it back before I leave for Denver."

Denver. Like a bucket of ice-cold water on a flickering flame, Mason's enjoyment of the day's antics dissipated in a plume of smoke. As if someone had reversed the biblical scene of Jericho, his wall of reserve and self-protection rose again.

"It's okay," Jimmy offered.

Rebekah stood up and looked back toward Mason.

Amusement once again flickered in the blue eyes that met his. Her mouth quirked with humor. "It's a very pretty dress, Mason, but don't you think it's a bit small for you?"

Only the sounds of nature could be heard as he processed her comment. Birds flittered and chirped in the overhanging trees. The gentle ripple of water cascading over rocks mingled with the *caw* of a lone crow.

"You gonna wear Mommy's dwess, Unca Mathon? Daddies don't wear dwesses."

Jimmy sucked back a loud snort and then exploded into a ball of laughter.

Rebekah's hand came up to stifle her giggle. Teasing laughter danced in her eyes.

"Yeah, Uncle Mason, you gonna wear that dress?" Jimmy slapped his leg and hee-hawed like the joke had been his idea.

Mason wadded the dress in one hand and tossed it toward Rebekah. He moved so fast in Jimmy's direction that the laughing boy didn't realize he'd been captured. "Let's go, Jim. You're gettin' a bath whether you want it or not."

"Wait." Instantly Jimmy's laughter died. "But I thought Rebekah was gonna take a bath. You gave her the dress. I don't want a bath," he yelled as Mason dragged him toward the creek.

❧

Rebekah watched Mason stomp toward the water. She fingered the pretty dress as she considered the kindness he'd offered. If she knew her teasing would have upset him so much, she'd have kept quiet.

Jimmy and Mason sat down along the creek bank and pulled off their boots. Mason helped Jimmy out of his clothes and then rolled up his own pant legs. Mason stood, never releasing his hold on his nephew. Rebekah smiled at Mason's lily-white legs covered in dark hair, wondering when they'd last seen the light of day. Yanking Jimmy up into his arms, Mason waded out into the knee-high water and gently tossed the boy in.

Jimmy's squeal rent the air until a loud splash drowned it

out. When she felt a tug on her pants, Rebekah look down at Katie.

"I wanna baff, too."

A bath sounded delightful. Rebekah looked down at her dirty, sweaty clothes. How nice it'd be to get out of these pants and back into a cool dress. When they'd pulled alongside the creek an hour ago, Mason declared they were taking a day off to rest the animals. The first thing Jimmy had done was drag his quilt to the creek and wash it out.

Rebekah eyed the water again. Even if she didn't take a bath now, she could wash Katie and enjoy the water's coolness on her hot feet. Maybe Mason and Jimmy could keep an eye on Katie during her nap, while she walked farther down the creek and bathed. Rebekah put the green dress in the back of the wagon, then walked back to the fire to stir the stew.

"Webekah, can I wash up, too?"

Rebekah smiled at the youngster. She was becoming very attached to the little girl. Pushing back the pain she'd face when leaving for Denver, Rebekah took Katie's hand and started for the water. "Sure, sweetie, let's give you a bath."

Katie tiptoed into the ankle-deep water and flopped down. Rebekah eased down on the creek bank and removed her boots and socks. Jimmy's squeals split the air as Mason flipped water at him. Rebekah grinned. It looked like Mason was getting wet after all, as Jimmy splashed back at him. Mason took another step in, and the water covered his knees.

Suddenly Rebekah got an urge she couldn't resist. She put her finger to her mouth, silencing Katie, and tiptoed into the creek. She resisted the urge to cry out when she stepped on a sharp rock. The cold water stung the blisters on her feet and sent goose bumps racing up her legs and onto her arms.

Easing up behind Mason, Rebekah held her breath. She caught the excited glint in Jimmy's eyes as she sucked in a deep breath and gave Mason the shove of his life.

"Hey!" he yelled as he landed in the creek, creating a huge

splash that washed Jimmy several feet downstream. Katie's laughter warmed Rebekah's heart just as Mason surfaced and turned a dark glare on her. *Uh-oh.* A spark of amusement instantly kindled in his eyes, turning into a blaze. Like a wild stallion tossing his thick mane, Mason shook his shoulder-length black hair, sending sun-glistening droplets of water cascading in every direction.

"Seems I was destined to take a bath today after all." A flash of humor crossed his face, and his mouth twitched with amusement.

Katie clapped her hands. "Unca Mathon got washed up."

Mason smiled at her; then his eyes narrowed. "What do you think, Katie? Think Miss Rebekah needs to get washed up?"

Rebekah's smile melted even as her heart gave a small leap. *He wouldn't dare.*

"Yep." Katie giggled. "Mith Webekah needs to get washed up." Rebekah turned her head to see Katie toss a handful of water at her.

A dark blur entered her side vision, and she turned to see Mason charging toward her. How could such a big man move so fast? Rebekah's eyes widened and she felt frozen to the spot. A scream tore at her throat, and she heard Jimmy's cackling laughter as Mason scooped her up and turned back toward the water.

"No, please, Mason, I'm sorry. Really, I am." Mason's breath warmed her face. His playful but roguish grin told her she'd get no mercy from him. Rebekah clung to Mason's damp shoulders, hands locked behind his neck, determined if he was going to toss her in, he'd go with her. His dark hair curled at his neckline, dripping tiny droplets of water on Rebekah's arm.

She felt her backside chill as Mason eased into the deeper water. When she saw Jimmy following, she looked up at Mason and indicated him with a nod of her head. Mason stopped and turned.

"Jimmy, it's too deep for you here. Move back there and keep an eye on Katie. I have business with Rebekah."

"Oh, shucks!" Jimmy commented.

Rebekah saw the boy turn back and felt relieved. She looked up at Mason, who'd stopped walking. His eyes glinted with mischief. This was a side of Mason Danfield she could easily learn to love. *Love? Where did that thought come from?*

"I predict Miss Rebekah's 'bout to take a plunge." His dark eyebrows bounced up and down in eager playfulness.

Rebekah took a deep breath, hoping to get her tumbling emotions under control. Being in Mason's arms was something she could easily get comfortable with. Did he have any idea the effect he had on her?

"If I go in, I'm taking you with me," she ventured.

Mason's eyebrows arched in skepticism. "Is that a threat?"

Rebekah pushed up, tightening her grip around his neck. "No, it's a promise."

Mason flashed a grin that could light a moonless night sky, and Rebekah's stomach churned at his nearness. He leaned his face closer to hers, and she thought for a moment he was going to kiss her.

"We shall see," he whispered.

The next moment, Mason gave her a hefty toss in the air and yanked his head from her frantic embrace. Rebekah landed with a splash about three feet away. Coldness gushed over her body, taking her breath away. Her feet slipped on the muddy bottom, and she sank down, hearing Mason's laughter booming through the air.

Rebekah managed to get her head above water and cried, "Mason," before she was sucked down again. Once again she broke the surface, searching, clawing for Mason. "Can't swim!" she yelled as once again she sank down.

Strong hands lifted her out of the water, and Mason pulled her against his chest. "I'm sorry, sugar, I didn't know you couldn't swim."

Rebekah took a deep, shuddering breath. As Mason took a step back toward the bank, Rebekah snagged her foot around his leg, causing him to lose his balance. In the next instant, Katie screamed as Mason and Rebekah hit the water together, a tangled mass of arms and legs.

Breaking the surface first, Rebekah shoved Mason back down. He grabbed her waist and lifted them out of the water together. Rebekah threw her head back and laughed. It had been so long since she'd felt this free and full of joy.

"Rebekah!" Mason's harsh voice cut into her joy like a dull knife. "That wasn't funny. Never joke about something as serious as drowning."

Setting her down in the water, he grabbed her by the arm and roughly pulled her to the shore. "C'mon, Jimmy, you're clean enough. There's work to be done."

Rebekah watched Mason jerk his socks on, stuff his feet into his boots, and stomp off. *Why would a little horseplay affect him so?*

Jimmy splashed toward the bank. He paused beside her, wiping the dripping water from his face. "Don't be mad at Uncle Mason. He's just upset. Mama and Aunt Annie drowned when a flash flood raced through the creek they were crossing."

Rebekah stared at the little boy as he trudged to the bank, grabbed a towel, and dried himself. She glanced down at Katie's stricken, tearstained face.

"Oh, sweetie, I'm sorry. Did I scare you?"

Katie nodded, wiping at her cheeks with a pudgy hand, smearing dirt and tears. Rebekah pulled the little girl into her arms.

Remorse stormed through her being. Just the other night Mason explained how his wife and sister had died. How could she have forgotten so quickly?

Oh, Lord, she prayed, *what have I done?*

eight

Mason sat on the ground, rubbing the oil into the leather harness with more force than necessary. His heart had finally returned to a normal beat after Rebekah's stupid stunt. Through narrowed eyes, he glanced up to watch Jimmy moving the horses, one at a time, to a new grazing area. He sighed a deep breath of relief that they'd finally found water.

Peeking out from under his hat, he glanced over to where Rebekah sat under a tree. Katie lay next to her on her quilt, sleeping. Mason stifled a grin at the sight of Jimmy's freshly washed quilt lying over a bush, drying in the sun.

Mason's gaze drifted back to Rebekah, his emotions swirling faster than a cyclone. Rebekah had gone downstream and bathed after putting Katie down for a nap. Now she sat there, wearing Danielle's dress and drying her waist-long hair in the sun as she used yellow thread to sew the hair back on Katie's dolly.

She was kind that way, doing little things that were important—things he'd never think to do. He couldn't help smiling when he thought how pleased Katie would be to see that her doll had sewn-on hair and blue-button eyes again. In her grief over her mother's death, the young girl had chewed the original buttons off.

Glancing down at his shirt pocket, Mason raised his hand to finger it but decided he didn't want to get oil on it. Last night Rebekah had asked him for his shirt—the one with the torn pocket. She'd washed it and laid it over a bush to dry overnight. This morning she took out her little tin box and stitched up the corner where it had flopped over for as long as he could remember. She even replaced the missing button. Afterward she made him change into it so she could wash his other shirt.

Rebekah laid Katie's doll aside to run the brush through her long tresses. Mason wanted more than anything to go over and take the brush from her hand and brush her hair. Evidently it was dry, because Rebekah set the brush down and began braiding. It amazed Mason that she could braid it behind her back. He still couldn't braid Katie's right even after lots of practice, but there sat Rebekah deftly plaiting her hair without even seeing what she was doing. After getting it started at the base of her neck, Rebekah pulled the thick, trifold cord over her shoulder and continued until she ran out of hair. Pulling a dark green ribbon from her pocket, she tied it off and flipped it back around behind her. He liked this version of Rebekah. Her hair wasn't hidden behind some dirty hat, and she looked quite feminine wearing a pretty dress instead of those old farmer's clothes.

When she wasn't being stubborn or foolish, Rebekah was an amazing woman. Her cooking, though not as delicious as Annie's, tasted good and warmed his belly. She had more patience with the kids than Annie. Mason shook his head. *Why am I comparing them?*

A warm breeze tugged at his hat, and Mason had to reach up quickly to keep it from sailing away. The children's clean clothing, drying on the nearby bushes, floated to the ground and lay in the dirt. Rebekah squealed and jumped up, chasing after them as the wind lifted them again and blew them out of reach. Mason grinned as she zigzagged from a shirt to a tumbling sock, then chased down a towel.

Danielle's green dress fluttered in the wind, grabbing at Rebekah's ankles. She looked good in green, even though the dress hung more loosely on her than it had on his sister.

"I don't suppose you could help," Rebekah said, shaking the dirt from the shirt in her hand. "All my clean laundry is getting dirty. Where did this wind come from?"

Mason grinned and held up an oily palm. "Got dirty hands. Didn't figure you'd want oil on your clean clothes." He set aside the harness and grabbed a rag, wiping his hands as he stood. Another stiff breeze snatched up his hat, then dropped it next to one of the wagon's wheels. Mason glanced upward. He'd been so focused on studying Rebekah, he hadn't noticed the dark, grayish green clouds streaming across the sky.

"Look's like a storm is brewing."

"We've got to get these clothes inside," she said, snatching up a pair of Katie's undergarments. "How can the weather change so quickly?"

"It does that here in the heart of the country. You'll be swimming in the creek one day and wake up to snow on the ground the next." Mason tapped down his hat and grabbed a pair of his pants as the wind whipped them against his leg. He gave them a sharp shake, and dust flew past on the stiff breeze.

Together they dumped the pile of clothing in the back of the wagon. "I need to make sure the horses are secured." Mason pointed toward the campfire. "You gather up all the loose things and get them in the wagon. I don't like the look of those clouds."

Rebekah looked skyward and her brow creased. She turned her gaze back toward him, and he saw the unspoken concern etched in her face.

"Uncle Mason!" Both their heads jerked toward Jimmy's frantic voice as he raced toward them. "Look!"

Mason and Rebekah hurried around the wagon to look in the direction Jimmy was pointing. Mason's stomach knotted as he took in the swirling, churning black mass of clouds ripping the earth apart as it cut a crooked path across the countryside. Rebekah's fingers clutched his arm, sending shafts of pain racing toward his shoulder.

He loosened her frantic grip and turned her to face him. The breeze whipped the shorter tendrils of her hair loose from her braid. A small, wind-tossed stick slammed against her cheek, and Rebekah jerked her head and grimaced. Her eyes, squinting against the flying dust, gazed up at him with near panic.

The cyclone roared closer. Its screams reminded Mason of a train barreling down the track. He leaned close to Rebekah's ear. "It'll be okay. Get Katie."

❧

Rebekah's heart raced faster than a wild mustang. She'd never been so afraid in all her life. Even marriage to Giles Wilbur didn't seem so awful at the moment. The closer the twisting black monster came, the more she shook. Her cheek stung from the debris flying around, slapping her face.

Mason's fingers cut into her arms. She turned to face him again. A depth of concern she'd never before seen enveloped his features. "Did you hear me?" he yelled. "Get Katie!"

Katie.

Instantly spurred into action, Rebekah raced toward the sobbing child. She scooped her up and turned around. Mason had Jimmy in his arms, racing toward her.

"The creek," he yelled, his black hair flying in all directions, making him look like some majestic warrior. Jimmy clung to him, his face buried against Mason's chest.

Mason's hand grasped her upper arm, pulling her toward the creek. Rebekah fought against her skirt, whipping in the wind, entangling her legs. She stumbled. Mason lifted her, dragging her forward. Rebekah clutched Katie with a death grip, lest the girl be ripped from her arms. The cyclone roared behind her, a heinous, black creature seeking to devour them. Cracking tree limbs splintered nearby. Rebekah ducked and ran faster.

A horse's terrified whinny stabbed at her heart as the earth rumbled when the large animal galloped past. Katie clung to Rebekah's neck with trembling arms. She held on so tightly, Rebekah felt her skin tingling with numbness, but with the cyclone bearing down on them, she couldn't take the time to loosen the child's grasp. Besides, the girl was terrified. Rebekah could hear her wailing cries over the howls of the wind. She could feel Katie's tears warm and wet on her shoulder.

Reaching the creek bank, Mason turned them south. He hurried along the water's edge, steadily urging Rebekah forward. When she stumbled again, nearly dropping Katie, his strong grasp hoisted her up and urged her to run. She ran on coltish legs, her fear spurring her on. Finally, when it seemed like the cyclone might overtake them, they rounded a bend. Here, past floodwaters had dug out a four-foot-high section of the bank, making a natural shelter, and Mason pulled them to the ground on dry dirt.

Rebekah peeked around Mason's arm. She couldn't see the monster, but its presence was evident. The shallow water whipped about as if struggling to escape its banks. Tree limbs, Jimmy's quilt, and their wooden bucket flew by. Thanks to their earthen shelter, the worst of the wind skittered around them. Grateful for his masculine strength, Rebekah turned her cheek into Mason's shoulder, shutting out nature's fury.

He set Jimmy down next to Rebekah, with a reassuring ruffle to the boy's head. Leaning over, Mason gave Katie a kiss on top of her head. His black eyes held Rebekah captive, urging her to be brave. Suddenly Mason jumped to his feet then leaned down toward Rebekah. His lips, warm against her ear, sent chills tunneling down her spine. "Need to check horses. Stay here. But get out—no matter what—if the water starts to rise."

Rebekah practically tossed Katie into Jimmy's arms. Turning, she grabbed at Mason's ankle. "No! Don't go!" His boot slipped out of her grasp. Rebekah squinted into the gray darkness, but Mason was already gone.

She turned back to the sobbing children and sheltered them with her body. A cold, stinging rain pelted her back, seeping into her dress.

Oh, Lord, watch over Mason. Keep him safe. Please.

After what seemed like an eternity, though Rebekah knew it was only minutes, she dared to raise her head. The sky had brightened, and the wind diminished. As quickly as the storm had come, it was gone, the rains reduced to a mist.

Pushing her hair out of her face, she checked the children. They were wet and visibly shaken, but they were alive and unharmed. *Thank You, Lord.*

Katie jumped into her arms, burying her face against Rebekah's chest. "Shhh, it's okay, sweetie. The storm's passed us. God kept us safe."

Jimmy started to shinny up the bank, but Rebekah snagged his pant leg and pulled him back. She smoothed Katie's damp hair from her face. "Katie, sweetie, go to Jimmy for a few minutes. I need to check things before you two come out."

"Aw, Rebekah, let *me* go," Jimmy pleaded. "I can check things."

Katie clutched Rebekah tighter, choking off her breath. She loosened Katie's arms. "Sweetie, come on, I need to have a look around and make sure the storm's over. Jimmy will hold you for a few minutes; then I'll be right back for you."

"But where's Unca Mathon? Did he get blowed away?" Her bottom lip trembled as she put words to Rebekah's own fears. Tears cascaded down Katie's cheeks, mingling with the rain and mud already streaking her face.

If Mason were okay, surely he would have returned for them by now. But he wasn't back, and she didn't hear him calling. What if he was hurt? Rebekah's concern for him grew by the second.

"Don't go, Webekah." Katie's sobs wrenched her heart even as her little arms strangled Rebekah's neck again.

"I'll be right back. I promise."

"Mama didn't come back."

Rebekah looked at Jimmy's wide-eyed stare. His black eyes looked so much like Mason's.

"C'mon, Katie," he finally squeaked out. "I'll hold you till Rebekah comes back."

Giving Jimmy a smile of gratitude, Rebekah disentangled herself from Katie's death grip. She rose to her feet, futilely brushing the dust and wrinkles from Danielle's dress. Standing on her tiptoes, she gazed over the top of their sanctuary, stunned at the destruction and disarray of their camp. She looked down at the children and smiled then turned and walked back alongside the peaceful stream. The calm water rippled along, belying the mayhem of the storm. In the far distance, Rebekah watched the cyclone continue its black path of destruction, the ever-hungry monster seeking other innocent, unwary victims to devour.

The canopy over the wagon, split in three pieces, rippled in the light breeze like an embattled flag. Thankfully, the wagon still stood, a brave survivor of the destruction. Ironically, Rebekah's pot of stew still sat over the campfire. She stared, amazed that the small fire had withstood the sudden, vicious downpour. Her clean clothes dotted the ground along the cyclone's path. The one thing she longed to see eluded her scope of vision.

Where is Mason?

Most of the trees in the area lay eerily on their sides. Those still standing resembled besieged soldiers with broken arms. In the field across the trail, Rebekah could see two of their horses grazing on the knee-high prairie grass as if nothing had happened.

Mason must be looking for the other horses.

Rebekah decided the most important thing she could do was secure the horses, but first she had to tend the children.

"Jimmy," she called from the ledge up above them, "bring Katie on up here."

Immediately she heard the children running along the creek bank, and then they scrambled over to her. Wide-eyed, they stared in amazement at the destruction. Katie wrapped her arm around Rebekah's leg, her dolly tucked in her other arm and her thumb in her mouth. Jimmy scanned the area, running his fingers through his hair just like Mason did whenever he was nervous or deep in thought.

"Where's Uncle Mason?" He turned to her with panic written all over his face. "Is he gone?"

Rebekah had hoped to see him returning by now and nearly voiced her worry, but she had to be strong for the children. She couldn't let them see that she was wondering the same thing.

"I figure he went looking for the other two horses. We need to get busy and clean up as much as we can before he gets back. He'll be so proud of us."

Jimmy straightened, as if in agreement.

"I want you two to stay together. Jimmy, you watch out for Katie. There may be sharp things around like broken tree limbs. You two start by gathering up all the clothes and putting them in the back of the wagon. Then stock up a pile of wood and set it near the campfire. I'm going to run over there"—she pointed to the field behind the wagon—"and bring back the two horses. Okay?"

Katie tightened her grip on Rebekah's leg. "I wanna go wif you."

Stooping down, she gave Katie a hug, then pulled a leaf from her hair. "Sweetie, I'll need both hands to bring back those two big horses. I need you to help Jimmy. It's very important that we find all of our clothes and other belongings before dark. It will be like a treasure hunt. Can you do that for me?"

Katie's eyes sparkled. "I can find tweasure. And Molly can help, since she gots eyes now." Touching a chubby finger to each eye, Katie turned Molly away from her. "See, Molly, there's Unca Mathon's shirt." Running over to the blue plaid shirt, she snatched it up and turned a victorious smile toward Rebekah.

"Good job, Molly, Katie. Go on, Jimmy, get busy and help Katie and Molly." Jimmy rolled his eyes as if he were too mature to partake in Katie's game.

"Watch her carefully," Rebekah whispered for his ears only. "I'll be back as soon as possible."

He nodded and turned, taking Katie by the hand.

Rebekah hurried toward the horses, slowing as she got

closer so as not to spook them. She recognized the closest horse as Mason's lead horse, Duke. Rather than wrestling with two of the huge animals, she grabbed the rope attached to Duke's halter and tugged him back toward the wagon. He came willingly with a soft whinny. Rebekah wondered if he was thankful for the human companionship. She tied Duke to one of the few trees still standing and turned back to get the other horse.

Scanning the countryside, she again wondered where Mason and the other horses were. As she neared the second horse, Rebekah spied a patch of red against the raw browns and dusty hues the tornado had left behind. A sudden sense of foreboding assaulted her so strongly she could almost smell it. Inching forward, she felt the blood drain from her face, causing it to go nearly numb. Raising a trembling hand to her mouth, she fought back the scream that sought so viciously to escape.

No! Mason!

nine

Rebekah slumped to the ground, ignoring the wetness saturating her dress. Mason's shoulder bulged upward in an unnatural manner. She doubted it was broken—maybe dislocated—but panic swarmed her mind at the sight of it. How could she fix a dislocated shoulder?

With trembling hands, she reached under her skirt and tore off a strip of her petticoat. She dabbed the blood on Mason's forehead, thankful when she realized the injury was only a small gash.

"Mason," she called, gently jostling his good shoulder. *Oh, Lord God, please help us.*

A moan erupted from somewhere deep inside Mason, softly reverberating through his body. Pain etched his face as he struggled to open his eyes. His eyelids fluttered then closed again as if the effort were too difficult. He lifted his good arm and squeezed his forehead, then reached for his wounded shoulder. "Ahh!"

Rebekah saw a muscle twitch in the side of his jaw as he gritted his teeth, and she clenched her jaw in sympathy.

"Shhh. I'm here, Mason. Try to relax and tell me how I can help you." Rebekah brushed his dark hair off his forehead, then ran her hand down his cheek.

"My arm—knocked—out of joint."

Rebekah dabbed at the sheen of sweat covering Mason's forehead.

"Gotta pop it back—happened before." Mason's chest rose in staccato rhythm as he sucked in short gasps of breath.

Rebekah felt a woozy darkness threatening to overpower her. This couldn't be happening again. A picture of her pale mother and little brother lying on their deathbeds, burning up with fever, haunted her. If only there'd been a doctor nearby. And here she was again, out in the middle of nowhere with Mason injured and maybe dying. Rebekah looked all around her. She didn't even know in which direction the nearest town was. She raised her hands to her face as unshed tears burned her eyes and tightened her throat.

No, God, please don't do this to me again.

"Bekah—I'm okay." She felt Mason's warm, calloused hand gripping her wrist. "It happened before. Help me—pop it back."

Rebekah spread her fingers apart and peeked at Mason. He didn't sound like he was dying. She took a deep, shuddering breath. "I don't know what to do."

"Put your foot—in my underarm. Grab my arm and jerk it—back in place."

"No, I can't do that. It'll hurt you." She laced her fingers together and pressed her hands to her mouth. The thought of bringing Mason more pain made her want to jump up and run away, just like she'd done when Curtis said she had to marry Giles Wilbur.

"And who knoweth whether thou art come to the kingdom for such a time as this?" The words she had read that morning from the book of Esther burst into her mind. Rebekah dropped her hands to her lap and sat up straight. Could everything that had happened to her have been God's plan to bring her to this exact place? What would Mason have done if he'd gotten hurt like this when he was alone with the children? Maybe she could redeem herself by helping them. The thought gave her courage. Even though she was on her way to Denver, it blessed her that God could use her along the way to help this man and the children. Swallowing back her remaining fear and doubt, she glanced up and met Mason's pain-filled gaze.

He lifted his head off the ground as if he needed to get closer to her. "I need your help, Bekah."

Bekah. That was the second time he'd called her Bekah,

and he'd never called her that before. It seemed almost as if saying her full name took too much effort. How could she not help him?

"Tell me what to do." She heaved the words with a heavy sigh. A smile tilted Mason's lips, bolstering her courage.

She slipped around to his wounded side, then sat down and removed her boot. Gently she eased her toes into Mason's warm underarm, the heel of her stocking instantly absorbing the moisture of the damp grass underneath. He grimaced, whether in real pain or anticipation, Rebekah wasn't sure. Wrapping her hands around the wrist of his useless limb, she gazed into his eyes. "I'm afraid I'll hurt you," she whispered.

"You can't hurt me any more than it hurts now." His eyes begged her for understanding. "Yank hard or you might have to do it again—and we don't want that, do we?" He gave her a weak smile and laid his head back down on the wet ground.

"How hard?" Rebekah didn't like the way her voice trembled. She needed to be brave for Mason's sake.

"Hard." The gritty tone in his voice left her no doubt.

"Wait," she cried. Reaching under her skirt, she tore another strip off her petticoat, then folded it into a square. "Bite down on this. Maybe it will help."

"Thanks." Mason's sweet grin sent her stomach turning flip-flops—or maybe it was just the sight of his abnormal-looking shoulder. Mason opened his mouth, and she laid the pad of cloth between his teeth.

"You ready?"

Mason stared deeply into her eyes, as if fortifying her for the task ahead. After a moment, he gave a brief nod.

God, help me do this right the first time—for Mason's sake.

Anchoring her foot into Mason's armpit, she gave him a final glance. His eyes were shut, dark eyebrows drawn down, and teeth clenched tightly on the fabric. Rebekah tightened her grip around Mason's forearm. She closed her eyes, heaved another quick prayer, and yanked with all her strength.

"Ahhh!" he cried out. His head dropped to the ground.

"I killed him!" Rebekah dropped Mason's arm and rose to her knees. Leaning over his still form, she cradled his face in her hands. "Please don't die," she whispered, patting his clean-shaven cheeks. Tears from her eyes dripped down onto his face and the backs of her hands.

In that moment, Rebekah suddenly realized how deep her feelings for Mason ran. She blinked in surprise. Though he irritated her with his stubbornness, she knew she'd never felt this way for a man before. Did she love him? How could she tell? She'd never known the love of a man—only Davy. But he wasn't a man, just a boy. And even though she cared for Mason, she knew he didn't love her. He still grieved for Annie.

She told herself to remember that God had put her here to help Mason and the kids through this rough time, not to fall in love. The thought brought more tears gushing forth. Tears of gratitude that she could be here to help. Tears of sorrow that Mason could never feel for her what she felt for him.

He uttered a soft moan, and his breathing returned to normal. With her thumbs, Rebekah wiped her tears off his face. She brushed back a lock of his damp hair and ran her fingers over his scalp, checking for other injuries. Mason heaved a deep sigh.

"Mmm. Do that again." Rebekah's hands halted. He was alive—and conscious? "Don't stop, Bekah. That feels great."

Staring at him in confusion, she leaned back, sitting on her heels, and wiped the tears from her face. The deeply etched pain no longer contorted Mason's handsome face. Instead, he seemed almost at peace. She glanced at his shoulder, relieved it no longer held that unnatural shape. She'd done it. A smile of pride tickled her lips and swelled her chest. In spite of her fear and insecurities, she'd held her ground, she hadn't run away, and Mason seemed better.

"Where are the kids?" He peeked out one eye for a moment then shut it again.

"They're picking up." She glanced back toward camp then realized she couldn't see the campsite because of the wagon.

At least the wagon had served to keep the children from seeing Mason on the ground.

"You're not hurt?"

"No, I'm fine." Rebekah glanced over her shoulder and saw that the horse still grazed nearby. "Do you think you could get on the horse so I could get you back to camp?"

He shook his head. "No, I'd be better off walking. You can help me if I need it."

"All right." Rebekah put her boot back on, trying to ignore her soaked stocking, and rose to her feet, taking a moment to brush off her dress while she willed her legs to stop trembling. Grimacing, Mason used his good arm to push himself into a sitting position. Rebekah noticed his gaze drift down to his wounded arm, which hung useless at his side. He'd need a sling or something to support his shoulder until it could heal. For now, she could stick his arm inside his shirt.

Kneeling back down, she undid the button she'd just sewn on his shirt—had it been only this morning? It seemed so long ago. Mason's eyebrows lifted in surprise, and a cocky grin tilted his lips.

"I've still got one good arm. I think I can tend to my own dressing."

Rebekah felt her cheeks flame. Lowering her eyebrows in a challenging glare, she picked up his wounded arm and stuffed his hand inside his shirt.

"Ow! You're brutal, Doc." Though Mason's words sounded gruff, she could see the teasing glint in his eyes. Eyes that reminded her of black onyx.

"Sorry," she murmured.

"Oh, yeah, I can tell you're real sorry." Mason nodded his head and rubbed his shoulder.

Rebekah nibbled on her bottom lip. She really didn't mean to hurt Mason, but sometimes his teasing irritated her as much as his stubbornness. He had no idea how much his being hurt had rattled her and brought back memories of her failure to keep her mother and Davy alive.

"Hey, I'm okay." Mason reached out, touching her cheek. "You did good, see? My shoulder still hurts, but I'm better."

She gave him a weak smile and shrugged her shoulders. "I. . .uh, need to wrap your head. Your cut's still bleeding." She took the two pieces of frayed cloth that she'd ripped from her petticoat and quickly formed a head bandage.

"Where're the other horses?"

"Duke's at camp. I don't know about the other two." She glanced down to see Mason staring off in the distance, his mouth cocked in frustration. "Can we pull the wagon with two horses?"

"No."

His curt answer didn't allow for exceptions. Without the other two horses, they were either stranded or would be forced to abandon the wagon and most of their supplies. Rebekah exhaled a deep sigh. This would be a long day. As soon as she got Mason settled in camp, she'd have to go looking for the horses while there was still daylight. At least dinner still simmered on the campfire.

Rebekah helped Mason to his feet. He wobbled a bit then slung his good arm around her shoulders. "You okay?" she asked.

"Just a bit dizzy—and my shoulder aches, but that's normal."

"How many times have you dislocated it before?"

"Twice. One as a kid and once. . .uh, never mind." He tightened his grip on her shoulder. Rebekah's frame sagged from the weight of Mason's big body. With one arm around his waist, she used her other hand to help hold his injured arm against his chest. The going was slow as they stepped over and around all kinds of debris, from tree branches to a dead duck to a derby hat, uncrushed and in perfect condition.

Mason gave a chuckle. "Where do you suppose that came from? I think we're days from the nearest town."

"I don't know. The storm was so strange." Rebekah reached up and tucked a loose strand of hair behind her ear. "Things are torn up all over the place, and yet my stew still sits over the burning fire, untouched."

"Twisters do weird things." Mason stopped and looked down at Rebekah. "We were lucky, Bekah." His gaze roved over her face and rested on her cheek. Conscious of his gaze, she reached up to touch her face. Mason gently nudged her hand away and ran his finger across her cheek. "You have a scrape."

"It's nothing—not like your injuries." Chills raced down her spine as Mason fingered the area near her cut.

"Looks like you'll have a bruise. Uh, listen. . ." He stared off toward their campsite a moment, then turned back to her. "I'm really glad you were here. I don't know what would have happened to me and the children without your help." He slid his fingers down her cheek and around to her nape.

Rebekah's breath caught in her throat. She closed her eyes, enjoying the warmth of his hands on her skin. Her heart danced and her breathing hurried to keep pace. He had no idea what his touch did to her.

"Sugar?"

Her eyes flew open, expecting to see Katie nearby, but instead Mason was peering down at her with an enduring smile tilting his fine lips. His warm breath tickled her face as he leaned closer. His eyes nearly begged her for a kiss. Rebekah couldn't breathe. She studied his gaze, expecting to see a teasing glint. He leaned closer. Rebekah leaned forward to meet him.

"Hellooo in the camp," came the distant intruding call.

ten

Reluctantly, Rebekah forced her gaze away from Mason's mouth and turned to see two men coming down the trail. Her heart skidded to a halt. Curtis and Giles Wilbur! Like a frightened deer, her gaze darted for a place to hide. She couldn't have come this far only to be caught and taken back and forced to marry against her will.

"Ow, easy there." Mason flicked the wrist of his injured arm, forcing her to loosen her death hold on his arm. Rebekah realized just how hard she'd been gripping it. He looked down at her, and his expression darkened. "What's wrong?"

She looked back to the men. Both were riding horses she didn't recognize, and behind them, they led Mason's other two horses. A small measure of relief filled her knowing Mason and the kids wouldn't be stranded. She looked toward the creek. If she took off running now, she might be able to get away.

Oh, God, why now? Mason needs my help. The children need me. What do I do?

Mason loosened his grip on her shoulders and turned to look her in the face. "Tell me what's wrong, Bekah."

Avoiding his probing gaze, she looked back toward the two men. They were closer now. Suddenly she realized the men truly were strangers—not Curtis and Giles. Knee-sagging relief flooded her. *Thank You, God.*

"You know 'em?"

Rebekah shook her head. "For a moment I thought I did. But, no, they're strangers."

"C'mon." Mason wrapped his arm around her shoulders again. "Get me to the wagon. I need my rifle."

The men drew closer, moseying along, not seeming to be in any big hurry. Rebekah was grateful for that small fact. As Rebekah and Mason approached the wagon, Katie and Jimmy came into view.

"Nuh-uh," Jimmy said. "I don't care if I am dirty again, no one's making me take two baths in one day."

"Uh-huh. Webekah will. You's all dirty again." Katie stood with her hands on her waist, looking like a little mama. Suddenly she caught sight of them. "Unca Mathon. You's hurt." Worry tilted her slim blond eyebrows, and she raised Molly to her chest in a fierce hug.

"I'm okay, sugar. Don't worry."

Katie studied him a bit to see if he was telling the truth; then she looked to Rebekah. She flashed the little girl a reassuring smile, and Katie gifted them with a dimpled grin. She gave Molly a kiss and a hug. "See, Molly, Unca Mathon's only hurt a wittle bit."

"Popped out your shoulder again, huh?" Jimmy sounded like a knowledgeable old man as he tossed his wet and dirty quilt onto the wagon's tailgate. Rebekah bit back a laugh, not wanting to embarrass him. She helped Mason to where he could lean against the wagon; then she climbed inside and found the rifle. As she exited the back of the wagon and jumped to the ground, the two strangers ambled into camp.

Mason reached toward the rifle, but Rebekah pulled it away, shaking her head. He couldn't shoot one-handed. He gave her a questioning glare, but she cocked the weapon and aimed it at the men. Mason's glare turned into an expression of surprise. She thought she caught a hint of wonder in his dark eyes before he turned back to face the two men.

For once, she felt thankful for all the hunting Curtis had forced her to do. It had paid off—she now had a dead aim. She stepped in front of Mason where she could get a clear view of the strangers. Mason grunted a little moan of frustration, and Rebekah felt herself being pulled back beside him. He gave her another intense look, clearly letting her know she wasn't in charge, even if he was banged up.

"Jimmy, Katie, over here," Mason ordered. The children must have caught the warning in his voice, because they both hustled forward. "In the wagon." Mason nodded his head toward the Conestoga. Jimmy lifted Katie with a little help from Mason; then the boy scrambled in behind her. Both children ducked down and peered over the back of the wagon.

In spite of her nervousness, Rebekah pursed her lips together to hide her smile. She'd never seen either child obey so quickly or quietly. She wondered if it had more to do with Mason being hurt or the strangers.

"Howdy," said the older of the two men, who looked to be in his late sixties. "Looks like y'all got a nasty taste of that cyclone what passed through. You folks all right?"

Mason nodded. "Been better off before, but then again, we've been worse off, too."

The old codger chuckled. "I hear ya." He nodded his head back toward the two horses he was leading. "These wouldn't be yours, would they?"

"Matter of fact, they are. I'm much obliged for your re-turnin' 'em."

"We saw them hightailing it away from the cyclone and figured somebody down this way'd be lookin' fer 'em." The old man turned to the younger man, who looked to be in his mid-forties. "This here's Beau, my son, and I'm Sam Tucker. Y'all mind if'n we share your camp for the night?"

Mason looked down at Rebekah. She saw the wariness in his gaze. "I reckon that would be the neighborly thing to do, seein's as you brought my horses back. Come on down and sit a spell. I could use a good sit-down myself." Mason turned and looked in the wagon. "Jimmy, hop down and tend to the horses. Then get out to that field and fetch Hector back fore he wanders off."

Rebekah felt Mason's arm go around her shoulders, and she looked up at him. Lines of pain and fatigue etched his face. "Help me over to that tree. Think I'll sit and rest up a bit; then I'll help get the camp back in order."

She uncocked the rifle and slipped one arm around Mason's waist. She tried hard not to think of how nice it felt to be able to cling to Mason's solid body, not to mention how having his arm wrapped around her felt better than being tucked into a toasty bed on a freezing cold night. She shook her head. She couldn't afford to think thoughts like that. Denver was her future, not Mason. A sigh of longing slipped through her lips, and Mason tightened his grip on her.

He leaned his head down next to her ear. "You all right?"

How could she be all right with his warm breath tickling her cheek? She nodded, not daring to look up and be face-to-face with the man filling her thoughts. "I'm sorry about all this," he whispered. "I know my getting hurt will mean extra work for you. And having these two men around might make things tense."

Mason's concern sent a sudden warmth racing through Rebekah's body. She ventured an upward glance. She never knew what she'd see in Mason's black eyes. Sometimes he glared back, making her wish she were a turtle and could just crawl into her shell. Then other times, the looks he gave her sent her blood churning. The feeling rumbling through her body now fell into the latter category.

"I don't mind the work," she said on a shaky breath.

"You wouldn't," he said with a smile. "But you already do so much; I don't know what I'll do when you leave us."

Rebekah's smile faltered. All he was worried about was how he'd get along after she left? What about her? How would she ever get Mason Danfield out of her mind? She'd best start right now. She helped Mason ease down to the ground and lean back against the tree's rough trunk.

"Thanks," he mumbled.

Sam and Beau Tucker had dismounted and were leading their horses toward the creek. She started to walk away, then felt a tug on the rifle. Glancing down, she caught Mason's gaze.

"I'd best hang on to that till we know for certain what these fellows are about."

"You couldn't even use it if you had to," she countered.

"If I have to, I'll manage. You can't lug it all over camp with you."

Rebekah relinquished the weapon and turned to check her stew. A deep emotional exhaustion seemed to make each step harder to take than the next. She'd allowed herself to think Mason felt something for her, but now she knew the truth. No man had ever loved her, and no man ever would.

She stopped in front of the campfire, trying to find the strength to stir the stew. Between the storm, Mason's getting hurt, and her realizing the truth about her relationship with him, she just wanted to curl up and go to sleep, but she had too much work to do. Rebekah looked around the camp area. Her wooden spoon was missing.

"Can I get down now?" Katie yelled from the back of the wagon.

Rebekah forced her feet to move. A hug from Katie just might be what she needed to suck her out of her depression.

ʘ

Mason laid the rifle in his lap. Until he got to know these strangers better, he'd rather play things safe. He drew the rag from his pocket that he'd used to wipe the oil from his hands earlier. It would serve well to polish the rifle's wooden stock and maybe distract his company from the real reason it rested in his lap.

He watched Rebekah amble toward the fire. She looked tired. He couldn't imagine what he would have done if she hadn't been here. He admired her brave spirit. With just a bit of encouragement, she'd pushed back her fear and popped his arm back into place. With a little shrug, he tested his shoulder, instantly sorry when a sharp pain jolted his torso.

Sam and Beau Tucker had watered their horses and filled their canteens and were making their way back toward him.

Both men strolled under the tree's shade and flopped down on the ground.

"Whewee! That cyclone was a big un," Sam said.

"Yep," said Beau.

"The worst of it missed us," Mason said. "I got Bekah and the kids tucked in a shelter next to the creek and went to secure the horses. Next thing I knew, somethin' knocked me in the head. I'd just raised my arm to check my forehead when a branch or something hit me from behind." Mason left the rag lying on the rifle as he rubbed his aching shoulder. "Ain't too bad, though." Until he knew what these men were about, he thought it best not to let them know just how badly he was injured.

Katie skipped over with a tin cup, water sloshing everywhere. "Webekah says I'm s'posed to give you this."

Mason smiled and peered into the blue tin mug. Only about a half inch of water remained. He bit back a grin and swallowed it in one gulp. "Mmm, delicious. You reckon you could fetch me some more?"

Katie giggled. "I can't, but Molly will."

Mason smiled. "That would be fine. Tell Molly thanks."

"That's a cute kid you got there." Sam watched Katie skip off toward the water.

"Actually, she's my niece. Her name's Katie. The boy is Jimmy, my nephew." Mason resumed polishing his rifle.

"So is Molly your wife then?"

"What?" Mason looked up in surprise. "Oh, no." He grinned. "Molly is Katie's doll."

The three men shared a laugh as Katie, carrying Molly, tiptoed back with another cup of water.

"That's a mighty fine-lookin' wife you've got. Lost my wife a couple years back." Mason's gaze darted toward Sam, and he studied the old man's face, not sure how to respond to that. Probably just as well that they thought he and Rebekah were married. Mason's gaze drifted back to Rebekah. A smile tilted his lips. Life definitely would be interesting married to her. Too bad she was so dead set on traveling to Denver.

"Yup, I lost my Hazel, and Beau lost his ma."

"Yep," Beau echoed.

Mason looked at Beau. The man dressed in faded overalls had to be near forty. So far all he'd said was "Yep." Somehow Mason wondered if Beau wasn't a few turnips short of a bushel.

"Where y'all headed?" Sam asked as he rifled through his saddlebags.

"Up Tulsa way," Mason said. "We're looking for the kids' dad. The last letter I got from him was posted in Tulsa."

"Ya heard what's goin' on in the Unassigned Lands in the Oklahoma Territory?" Sam pulled a wad of beef jerky out of his bags and bit off a hunk, then handed it to Beau. He bit off a chunk and offered it to Mason.

Shaking his head, Mason tried not to grimace at the thought of eating after these two less-than-clean men. They looked like trappers who had been up in the mountains for years. "Hillbillies" is what folks in this part of the country called them.

Unassigned Lands. He'd heard about the lands originally plotted out for Indian reservations but never assigned to a specific tribe. Mason racked his brain, trying to think if he'd heard something about them lately. Finally he shook his head. "What's happening in there?"

"Ain't you seen a newspaper lately?"

Mason shook his head, not a little surprised that Sam could read. "Nope. Been travelin' awhile."

"Well, that new president of ours, Benjamin Harrison, signed a bill opening up the Unassigned Lands in Indian Territory for settlers. There's gonna be a big race—a land run. They's callin' it Harrison's Hoss Race."

"How's it work?" Mason asked, setting his rifle aside.

"The Land Run starts at noon on April 22. Folks can race for a lot in town or a 160-acre plot in the country. The paper says ya gotta register in either Guthrie or Kingfisher in the

Oklahoma Territory if you git lucky 'nough to stake a claim. Costs fourteen dollars. That's an awful lot, if'n you ask me."

Mason knew Jake would want in on the run. It was just the kind of opportunity he'd jump at. Jake probably wasn't even in Tulsa anymore—not if he knew about the Land Run. The problem was, he'd told Rebekah he'd drop her off in the first big town they came to. Of course, if they didn't stop in Tulsa, she'd have to continue traveling with them.

He looked across the campfire and watched Rebekah redo Katie's hair. She nibbled her lip and looked deep in thought. He glanced around to check on Jimmy. The boy, wearing the derby hat, was leading Hector back from the field where Bekah had found Mason.

Would that be fair to Bekah—to make her travel to the Oklahoma Territory? It *would* get her closer to her destination.

The truth was, he wanted to spend more time with her. He wasn't ready for her to leave. Of course, he needed her more than anything now that he'd been injured. Hadn't he heard that the train cut across the Territories from Kansas all the way down to Texas now? If they headed far enough west, they'd have to come across it sooner or later. Then she could catch the train up to Dodge City and on to Denver. Until then, he'd have time to heal and get himself ready to say good-bye.

Mason turned back to Sam. "You know if there's a train that crosses the Territories?"

"Yup. Yup. The Atchison, Topeka, and Sante Fe Railroad runs through there."

Stretched out on the ground beside Sam, Beau began snoring. The irritating noise reminded Mason of a badger's snarling growl.

Mason looked back at Rebekah, and a small grin tilted his lips. She and Katie had filled their arms with the tornado-tossed clothing they'd washed that morning. The two females were headed back to the creek, evidently to wash the clothes for the second time in one day.

"Yup, that's a mighty fine-lookin' woman you got there." Sam laid back, his head on his crossed arms, and closed his eyes.

Mason felt his ears warm, knowing the old man had caught him staring at Bekah. He forced away pleasant thoughts of having her for a wife. "How long you reckon it would take to get from here to the Territories?"

"You're already in Indian Territory, but I imagine it'd take less than a week on horseback from here to cross into the Oklahoma Territory. Course, pullin' a wagon the size of your'n, more likely two weeks."

"Got any idea what the date is?" Mason asked.

"Yup. Early April—somewheres around the fourth or fifth." Sam yawned and turned onto his side.

One-handedly, Mason calculated the days. That gave him barely two and a half weeks to get to Oklahoma before the Land Run—if they didn't stop in Tulsa. It wasn't like he'd promised Bekah they'd stop there, and sure as shootin', Jake would be off somewhere else once the Land Run was over. Mason couldn't afford to miss him.

Almost against his will, his gaze drifted back to Rebekah again. She wrung the water out of one of Jimmy's shirts then flipped a handful at Katie. His young niece giggled and whipped a dripping sock in the air, getting more water on herself than on Bekah. Rebekah unrolled Jimmy's shirt and gave it a ferocious shake. Katie squealed and ran back toward the creek bank. Mason chuckled.

He loved Bekah's playfulness. *Whoa! Loved? Where did that come from?* Mason ran his hand through his hair, suddenly wondering where his hat had ended up. Loved. It was simply a figure of speech, wasn't it?

Yeah, then why did you kiss her, Danfield?

Mason laid his head back against the tree trunk. He didn't want to have feelings for Rebekah. He had plans. Take Jimmy and Katie to Jake, then head west—alone. Suddenly, being alone didn't sound so great.

The sound of water splashing and Katie giggling tickled his ears. Songbirds had returned to the wind-tossed trees and were trying to outdo each other in their cheerful choruses. A gentle breeze tugged his hair. Maybe it would be best to take Rebekah to Tulsa after all.

But how could he manage without her now that he was wounded? He opened his eyes and studied the ground nearby. He reached out and snatched up a small rock. With a deep sigh, he heaved the rock to the far side of the camp, instantly regretting his sudden movement when pain riveted across his chest. The rock landed in the dirt near Duke. The big horse snorted and jumped, his brown hide quivering.

"Don't splash me, Katie. I'm warnin' you." Jimmy's stern tone drew Mason's gaze back to the creek. "I told you I've had all the water I want for one day."

"But you's dirty again," Katie reasoned.

"It's okay for men to be dirty."

"Nuh-uh. It ain't okay for anybody to be dirty." Katie stood ankle-deep in the creek with her dripping fists on her waist. " 'Sides, you ain't a man. You's just a boy."

"Well. . ." For once, Jimmy didn't seem to have the words to argue with his sister. "Well, I'm not gettin' wet—and that's final." He plastered his fists on his hips, daring Katie to argue more. Suddenly Hector lifted his dripping muzzle from the creek where he'd been drinking. The horse stepped toward Jimmy and nudged him in the back with his big head, sending the boy flying into the creek. Jimmy rose from the water, sputtering and fuming. Like an Indian on the warpath, he danced in the creek and glared at the horse. Good thing for Hector, Jimmy didn't have a tomahawk handy.

Mason's lips split into a grin, and he couldn't hold back his chuckle. Katie and Bekah howled with laughter. Jimmy whirled around, glowering at them both. Hector whinnied as if joining in the fun.

"You's did get two baffs in one day." Katie covered her mouth as she giggled.

Jimmy grabbed Hector's lead rope and led him out of the creek. "Some friend you are," Mason barely heard him mutter as the boy stomped away, dripping water everywhere.

Smiling, Bekah followed Jimmy out of the water. She shook open the boy's shirt and laid it across a bush. Cupping her palm over her eyebrows, she looked in Mason's direction. A warmth saturated his being. She was checking on him. He raised a hand in a little wave. A pale rose color stained Bekah's cheeks as she waved back. Bending down, she picked up one of his shirts and turned back toward the creek.

Mason laid his head back against the tree trunk. His eyelids drifted shut. Who was he kidding? He wanted Bekah around as long as he could manage. Just maybe, getting laid up was the best thing to happen to him in a long while.

eleven

"No, I'll do it. You just sit down and rest." Rebekah glared up at Mason, daring him to argue with her again. For the past two days, he'd been cranky, fussing to get back to work. The foolish man wouldn't lay still and allow his arm to heal. And, as if that wasn't enough, he'd been bossing everyone around as if they didn't know enough to do their chores without his oversight.

Mason's eyes narrowed. He seemed to be contemplating his response. "Look," he finally said, "I hurt my shoulder. I'm not dead or dying, Bekah. I don't need to be babied like an infant still in the cradle."

"Well, you don't need to be messing with the horses just yet either. It's only been two days since your shoulder was dislocated." She moved closer and tilted her head back farther to see clearly into his dark eyes. " 'Sides, I haven't been babying you."

Mason stepped forward, the toes of his boot knocking into her shoe as Rebekah tried to gulp down the knot in her throat. Knowing full well she had been doing everything she could to make his recovery easier, Rebekah now avoided his gaze and stared at the stubble on his chin. The very chin she had shaved just yesterday. Her heart had barely slowed its erratic throbbing from being so close to him and from rubbing her hands across his rough cheeks. She was so thankful he hadn't perished in the storm that she'd been willing to do almost anything to help him.

"I—I don't want you to hurt your shoulder," she whispered as she read the words *Blue Creek Mills* on the sling she'd made for Mason out of an old flour sack. He reached behind him and adjusted the sling against his neck.

"I told you this has happened before. I know my limits. You're gonna have to trust me on that."

"But the horses—" Mason's warm finger on her lips halted her next words. She swallowed, willing her heart to slow down. Being close to Mason like this was making Denver look less and less appealing.

"You and Jimmy can help me with the horses. I'm trying to be careful and not do too much, but you're gonna have to trust me." His eyebrows arched as if waiting for her to disagree.

Oh, but I do trust you. If you only knew how much.

"Hee-hee." Sam shuffled past them, chuckling and tugging on his faded suspenders. "You two's not gonna have a very happy married life if'n y'all argue all the time like that. Best y'all should just kiss and make up."

Rebekah felt as if her cheeks had caught fire. "They've been here two days, and you never told him we aren't married," she hissed at Mason.

Mason grinned at Sam, but his smile faded when he caught her glare. He looked like a schoolboy with his hand caught in the pickle barrel. He opened his mouth to say something then clamped it shut.

Straightening, Rebekah leaned toward Mason. "Well, if you won't tell him, I will." She swung around, mouth open ready to inform Sam of her unmarried status. "Sa—"

Mason's warm, calloused hand settled over her mouth, halting her words. He pulled her against his chest, holding her tight. Frustrated, Rebekah wanted to fight against him but was afraid she'd hurt his shoulder, so she allowed herself the luxury of leaning back against Mason's solid body.

Sam had stooped down to load his saddlebags and had his back to them. Beau was on the other side of the wagon, taking his horses to the creek, with Jimmy and Katie tagging along. Rebekah felt Mason's cheek against her head as he leaned down close to her ear. His nearness shot spikes of attraction up her spine. "At first, I didn't want them to know.

I thought it was safer for you that way." Mason's warm breath tickled her ear. "Then I decided not to tell them. I didn't want them getting any wrong ideas about us."

Rebekah snorted an unladylike laugh against his warm, salty hand, which remained lightly against her lips. What about the wrong idea that they were married?

Sam stood and turned. Mason released her mouth and ran his hand along her cheek; then he let it rest against her neck. She couldn't move. Could he feel her ferociously pounding pulse?

Sam chuckled. "Yup, making up's the best part, ain't it? Give the little woman a kiss for me, Mason." He grinned his gap-toothed smile and ambled toward the creek.

Mason tightened his grasp and leaned down, kissing Rebekah firmly on the cheek. She stiffened at his unexpected display of affection, then shoved her elbow in his belly. He *oompfed* a gasp of air then chuckled. "I'm just obeying my elders, sugar."

Rebekah grabbed his arm and yanked it away, then stomped off to finish packing the wagon. "Of all the nerve." She swatted at her cheek where it still burned from Mason's kiss. Tears stung her eyes. Why couldn't he kiss her for real, instead of making it a big joke? If only Prince hadn't given out on her, she'd be in Denver by now and Mason Danfield would be a distant memory. So why didn't that thought make her feel any better?

❧

Rebekah hadn't talked to Mason all day. She sat stiffly beside him on the wagon seat as if he weren't there. Mason lifted his hat, thankful he'd found it under a bush near their camp, and scratched his head. He couldn't for the life of him figure out what he'd done—unless it was the kiss. But he was just funnin', humoring Sam really. Surely she didn't take offense at something so harmless.

Sam and Beau had said their good-byes and trotted their

horses down the trail toward the Unassigned Lands. Actually, Sam had said good-bye and Beau had just said, "Yep." Mason racked his brain, trying to remember if Beau had said anything else the whole two days they'd spent together. The son was as quiet as his father was chatty—a strange but friendly pair.

Mason peeked out the corner of his eye at Bekah. She'd loosened her braid, allowing her long brown tresses to spread out over her shoulders like a soft cloak. Her hair reached all the way to the wagon seat. He wondered how she ever managed to stuff it all up under that silly felt hat she often wore. His fingers itched to reach out and touch her hair. Instead he tightened his grip on the reins.

If only she weren't so dead set on going to Denver. . .

Mason heaved a sigh as he realized his thoughts had ambushed him again. When had he started developing feelings for Bekah? Adjusting his hat, he sneaked another glance. She combed her fingers through her hair, then began rebraiding it. He turned his face forward, concentrating on the fly buzzing around Duke's head. It was either that or stare at Bekah like an enamored young pup.

The wagon jostled and squeaked down the dirt trail. The horses' hooves *clip-clopped* slowly in the soft dirt and prairie grass. Katie and Jimmy giggled from the back of the wagon as they used stick rifles and pretended to shoot the flock of crows that seemed intent on following them. Mason's right arm, still supported by Bekah's sling, felt hot against his chest as the warm afternoon sun beat down on them. He yawned. At least they were no longer fighting that blast of cold that had run in and pelted them with sleet and rain, then hurried back to the north like an ornery kid playing tag.

Mason slouched forward, resting his good arm on his knee, and closed his eyes. If things went right, in less than a week he'd find Jake, return the kids to him, and put Bekah on a train to Denver. He squeezed his eyes tighter, trying to determine which action would hurt the most. How had

Bekah managed to wind her way into his life so soundly? Into his heart? Maybe it was just because they were thrown together with no real choice in the matter. He couldn't exactly have left her alone on the prairie. Then when he got hurt, he needed her even more. He needed her. . . .

Mason clenched his jaw. He didn't need Rebekah. He was going west—alone. If he came to love Bekah, it would be just a matter of time before something took her away from him. And he couldn't endure losing the woman he loved a second time.

"Mason, are you in pain?" Bekah's hand warmed his shoulder where she touched him.

Pain. Yeah, but not the kind she meant. How could he say good-bye to Katie and Jimmy? To Bekah? Why couldn't something go right in his life—just for once? How far west would he have to go to outrun his pain?

"Mason? Are you all right?"

"Yeah. Fine," he grunted without looking at her.

"I just hope you aren't overdoing it."

Mason turned a glare on Bekah. "Don't mollycoddle me."

"I. . ." Bekah turned her head away, but not before he caught a shimmer of tears glazing her eyes.

Mason snapped the reins, sorry for losing his temper. The four horses had nearly slowed to a crawl as they pulled the heavy wagon up another round-topped hill. "He-yah! C'mon, Duke. Get a move on."

"I didn't realize I was babying you. I'm sorry." Bekah's soft whisper sent daggers of condemnation spearing into him.

Mason pressed two fingers against the bridge of his nose, chastising himself for taking his frustrations out on her. She was only watching out for his welfare. He turned in the seat to face her. "No, I'm sorry. I shouldn't take offense to your watching out for me."

She flashed him a brief, tight-lipped smile. "It's all right." Rebekah fiddled with her dress, folding a section in her lap and unfolding it. "How much longer do you think it will be fore we get to Tulsa?" She looked up at him, hopeful expectation glistening in her blue eyes. Mason's gut twisted when he saw her damp eyelashes clinging together in tiny spikes—or maybe it was because of what he had to tell her.

"Uh. . .we already passed Tulsa."

"When? I never saw it." Bekah's eyebrows scrunched together as if she were struggling to remember.

"We skirted around it yesterday. Sam told me it was quicker to get to the Oklahoma Territory going as the crow flies rather than turning off the trail to Tulsa."

Bekah nibbled on her bottom lip. "Those train tracks we crossed yesterday went to Tulsa?"

"Yeah."

"I could be heading for Denver right now."

Mason winced. Denver again. The woman obviously had a one-track mind. Why did he ever think she'd be interested in a life with him? "My mistake." There could be no confusing the tone of his voice. "I figured you'd want to stay on with us awhile longer—with me being laid up some."

Rebekah turned a hurt gaze toward him. "You could've at least asked me before deciding on your own. It was my choice to make."

She was right, but in the mood he was in, he didn't feel like giving her the satisfaction of admitting as much. Instead, he picked up her long braid and flicked it like a whip, then nudged her shoulder with his. "You know what your decision would have been anyway, right?"

She gave him an indistinguishable stare. Kind of like a hunter staring down a cougar.

"I'm helpless, remember?" He wiggled his eyebrows and the arm in the sling, ignoring the twinge of pain bolting through his shoulder.

Her pretty mouth twisted into a wry grimace.

Mason decided to pull one of Katie's stunts. "Don't be mad

at me, sugar." He pressed his lips into a pout.

Bekah maintained her stoic expression only a few seconds before she tucked in her lips in her effort not to crack a smile, but the sparkle in her eyes gave her away.

"We could always kiss and make up, like Sam suggested." Mason gave her an ornery grin then struggled to return his lips to a pout again.

Bekah crossed her arms over her chest and glared at him.

Mason heard a scuffling sound; then Katie popped her head out from the back of the wagon. "What's the matter? You sad, Unca Mathon?"

Bekah gave a little laugh that sounded like it came out of her nose.

"No, sugar, I'm not sad." He reached back and ruffled her already-messed-up hair. "Just playin' with Bekah."

"I gots ta go again." Katie stared up at him expectantly. He narrowed his eyes, trying to determine if she was telling the truth or just looking for a way out of the wagon. Katie looked at him with wide blue eyes; then her pink little lip pushed out into a darling pout.

Mason glanced up at Rebekah. Their gazes locked. Bekah's eyes twinkled with mischief, and she stuck out her lip at him. He couldn't hold back his howl of laughter. Bekah's shoulders bounced with her own mirth. Katie looked at them like they'd both gone crazy.

"Don't waff at me." Katie shook her head like an offended matron. "I gots ta go weal bad. Weally, Unca Mathon."

Mason and Bekah's laughter only increased. Tears blurred Mason's vision as he reached back and lifted Katie onto the wagon seat, ignoring the sting in his wounded shoulder.

Katie sat stiffly on the seat with her pudgy little arms crossed over her chest. "It's not funny," she huffed.

"What's not funny?" Jimmy poked his head up then grabbed Mason's arm. "Look there." He pointed over the horses' heads. Mason choked back his laughter at the sudden urgent tone in Jimmy's voice. Up ahead, a buckboard listed unnaturally to the left. A man squatted beside the broken wheel as if trying to decide what to do. They pulled up closer to the busted wagon.

Suddenly a woman stepped from behind a tree, her rifle pointed straight at them.

twelve

Rebekah's heart pumped with anxiety. Were they about to be robbed? Would they lose their wagon—or worse? Mason couldn't defend them with an injured shoulder. She breathed a quick prayer as she leaned forward and reached toward the rifle resting on the floor near her feet.

Mason firmly but gently grabbed her shoulder, giving her a quick shake of his head as he turned his gaze toward the strangers. "We don't mean you folks any harm. We'd like to help if we can."

The woman studied them for a long moment; then Rebekah sighed with relief as the older woman lowered the barrel of the rifle till it pointed at the ground.

"I don't reckon you'll do us harm if you got your wife and kids with you."

Rebekah groaned. *Not the wife thing again.* She sat up on the hard seat. First chance she got, she was going to set the woman straight.

"Come sit a spell. Maybe we could share dinner tonight," the woman offered. Suddenly the thought of talking with another adult woman tickled Rebekah's insides. She hadn't had a conversation with a woman since her mother died.

Mason clicked the horses forward then guided the wagon to the side of the trail. One-handedly, he helped Rebekah and Katie descend from the wagon. Jimmy hopped out the back and hustled around to the front. He started to unhitch the horses but stopped and looked at Mason for permission. Rebekah saw Mason give the boy a swift nod; then with the grace of a three-legged bear, Mason climbed down from the wagon. His jerky motions made her wonder how much his shoulder still hurt him. And she didn't miss the fact that he left the rifle on the wagon floorboard. Knowing he felt that comfortable already with these strangers eased some of the tension tightening her neck and shoulders.

Feeling a tug on her skirt, she looked down to see Katie's forlorn face. Rebekah bit back a smile at Katie's cross-legged dance. She grabbed the girl's hand and rushed her behind the wagon, grinning as Mason's soft chuckle followed on the warm afternoon breeze.

By the time they returned, the horses were grazing in the nearby field and Mason had squatted beside the man, looking over the broken wheel. Rebekah headed toward the woman, her arm jerking as Katie held her hand and skipped along beside her. The woman looked to be in her late fifties or so. Her plump figure amply filled out the faded blue calico. Graying brown hair was bunched in a loose bun at her nape, and a bonnet hung down her back with the tie forming a strange bow under the woman's two chins.

"Howdy! I'm right pleasured to meet you'ns. I'm Ella Robinson, and that's my Luther fixing the wagon wheel."

Rebekah smiled. The woman had kind blue gray eyes and a friendly grin. "This is Katie, and I'm Rebekah Bailey." Katie blessed the woman with a dimpled smile and a brief wave; then she tugged her hand free from Rebekah's and skipped off toward Jimmy, who had squatted next to Mason.

"Your Mr. Bailey was kind to offer us help. We's anxious to get back on the road to Oklahoma. Gonna get us some land in that big race they's gonna have there."

Rebekah watched Ella Robinson rustling around in the back of her wagon. She pulled out what looked to be biscuit fixings. Suddenly it dawned on Rebekah what the woman had called Mason. Mr. Bailey. She didn't know whether to laugh or scream, but she knew she had to set the woman straight. "We're heading there, too." Rebekah turned and pointed to Mason. "His name's Mason Danfield, and the boy is Jimmy. The children are Mason's niece and nephew." Rebekah cleared her throat. "And we aren't married."

Mrs. Robinson stopped almost in midstride. She looked at Mason and back to Rebekah. Her gaze darkened, and her thick lips thinned into a straight white line. "Oh, my. That's not at all proper." Her withered hand rose to her mouth.

Rebekah stepped forward and laid her hand on the woman's arm. "Please, it's not what you're thinking."

The woman's gaze looked skeptical. Rebekah's words rushed forth as she told the story of how Mason had rescued her, but she left out the part about how she'd run away from home—away from an unwanted marriage. Mrs. Robinson seemed to ponder her words for a moment, then shook her head. Before Rebekah could blink twice, the woman set her bowl of supplies on the tailgate and tugged Rebekah into her plump arms. "You poor thing. You must have been so frightened. Well, you're safe now. Luther and I'll take care of you. Since we're both goin' to Guthrie, you can travel with us."

Rebekah was flabbergasted. Not travel with Mason? But he needed her, didn't he? She felt a sudden warmth at her shoulder and knew instantly that it was Mason.

"Uh. . .that's mighty kind of you, ma'am, but you can see I'm laid up some and sure need Bekah's help, especially with the kids and the cookin'."

Mrs. Robinson gave Mason a thorough dressing-down with her eyes. Rebekah didn't think she'd like being on the wrong side of the older woman's temper, but she had to give Mason credit for not squirming. "I promise, I've been a perfect gentleman the whole time Bekah's been with us. Right, Rebekah?"

She was tempted to toy with his emotions a bit, but the look in his eyes told her that his reputation was too important to tease about. "Yes," she said, pushing away the thought of Mason's kisses. "He's been nothing but kind to me—probably even saved my life."

"Well, I supposed ya did what ya had to, given the circumstances." Mrs. Robinson's gaze softened a fraction toward Mason. "But since we're headed the same direction, Luther and I can be chaperones. That way, Rebekah can help you and sleep with us, and things will be all proper-like." Mrs. Robinson turned around and scooped up her biscuit fixings again, then pivoted back to face them. "Oh, and another thing, we're just plain ol' Luther and Ella."

Rebekah turned to study Mason's expression. Here was another situation he couldn't control. She wondered if he was fuming inside or if he was glad to be relieved of her. The muscle in his jaw twitched just before he spun away and stalked back to his wagon.

She didn't particularly like the change herself. Things had been going along just fine without the Robinsons chaperoning. Suddenly Rebekah's mind flashed back to the nighttime rainstorm when Mason and Jimmy had climbed in the back of the wagon to stay dry. She felt her cheeks flame. What would Ella say if she knew Mason had taken her in his arms and kissed her?

It probably was a good idea to put some distance between her and Mason—before her heart became any more entwined with him and the children. Each day of their journey brought them closer to their destination—and a train or stage that would take her to Denver and away from Mason forever.

Suddenly Denver didn't sound as appealing as it once had. Pushing those unwanted thoughts from her mind, Rebekah tucked a wisp of hair behind her ear and turned to Ella. "What can I do to help?"

☙

One week later, the roads near the border of the Unassigned Lands were thicker with people than a wheat field covered in a swarm of grasshoppers. Mason had never seen so many humans in one spot, not even back in Atlanta. Wagons of every kind and size parked along the sides of the road and across the fields. The air was thick with the odor of campfires, horses, and unwashed bodies.

Water was sure to be a problem with so many people congregating in such a small area. He felt thankful he'd had the sense to fill both of his barrels at the last creek they'd crossed.

"Have you ever seen so many tents and people?" Rebekah said, her voice filled with awe. "I never dreamed there'd be so many here."

"It's downright shocking, ain't it?"

Rebekah nodded. "I don't think I've ever heard so much noise before. I grew up in the woods. The only noise there is the sound of insects and the wind whipping through the tall pine trees."

A man clad in worn overalls whistled at a boy about Jimmy's age who ran across the path in front of the slow-moving wagon. Duke snorted and tossed his head then continued down the road. Tired-looking women seemed to be making camp the best they could under the circumstances. Mason felt a twinge of regret that Bekah would be subjected to living in these awful circumstances. Then again, she might be on the train to Denver by nightfall.

With Ella's close chaperoning, they'd hardly talked the past week. The only time they'd had together without the Robinsons was when Bekah rode with him on the wagon, and then the children were constantly vying for their attention. Mason didn't know how Katie would handle Bekah's leaving. He wasn't sure how he would handle it.

Maybe he should just ask her to stay. . .and do what? Travel west with him? Mason shook his head. He wasn't going to come between Bekah and her dream. And he wasn't going to let her come between him and his plans. It was better this way. He'd lost everyone he'd ever loved except Katie and Jimmy—and they'd soon be gone, too. If he gave Bekah his heart, it would only be a matter of time before something took her away. Better she should go now while she claimed only a portion of his heart rather than the whole thing.

"Where will we camp?" Rebekah's words jarred his thoughts.

"Let's see where Luther and Ella go." He pulled off his hat

and ran his fingers through his sweaty hair. "I'd like to camp with someone we know so they can help with the kids." *After you leave.* He couldn't voice the final words out loud.

"Maybe it won't be so crowded on the other side of town."

"Maybe."

The long screech of a train whistle screamed over the din of the crowd. Mason saw Bekah jump; then she turned to face him. Their gazes locked. The noise surrounding them faded as Mason sat captivated by Bekah's melancholy gaze. The reality of her leaving hit him in the gut. It almost seemed as if she didn't want to go. But probably she was just dreading saying good-bye to the kids. He could tell she loved them.

"Unca Mathon, what was that noise?" Katie's blond head popped up from the back of the wagon.

"I told her it was a locomotive, but she don't believe me," Jimmy said.

Mason chuckled. He doubted Katie even knew what a locomotive was.

"It sounded like a monk-ster," Katie said, her gaze darting in every direction.

Bekah reached back and patted the little girl's head. "Don't be afraid, sweetie. It's just a train. It won't hurt you."

"Why is there so many peoples here?" Katie asked.

"This is where they're having that Land Run Sam told us about. Right, Uncle Mason?" Jimmy sounded like a little man, trying to impress the ladies. Mason suppressed a smile.

"Nuh-uh. Land can't run, can it, Webekah?" Katie crossed her arms, looking to Rebekah for support. "It ain't gots no legs."

Mason's heart somersaulted at the way Bekah's eyes twinkled while she fought to keep from laughing. The wagon croaked and groaned down the trail as he watched her struggle to answer. After a moment, she seemed to have regained control.

"You're both right, Katie. The land doesn't have legs, so it can't run. But the race Jimmy mentioned is called a Land Run because people run to get free land."

"Water doesn't have legs, but it runs," Jimmy mumbled.

"Nuh-uh," Katie said.

"That's enough," Mason said, using his no-tolerance voice. "You two go watch out the back for a while. We'll be camping soon."

"Yes, sir," Katie and Jimmy said in unison; then they disappeared into the wagon.

Mason turned his back to Bekah. "Untie this thing, will ya?" His arm had been immobilized in the sling for nearly a week and a half.

"Are you sure you're ready to be using your arm?" Rebekah asked over his shoulder. Her warm breath tickled his cheek, doing strange things to his insides.

He pushed the feeling away. "There may be lots of rough people around here, and I don't want to seem an easy mark. I'll be careful. 'Sides, it hasn't hurt much the past few days. I've been moving it around some when you weren't watchin'."

Rebekah smacked him on his good shoulder; then her fingers fiddled with the knot, tickling the hair along his nape and sending shafts of excitement coursing down his spine. After a few moments, the sling fell loose around his chest, and his arm was free again. He carefully moved the stiff limb back and forth, testing his range of motion.

"See, good as new." He flashed Bekah a smile, hoping to prove his point.

She seemed to be observing him for signs of pain. Beyond her shoulder, a familiar figure darted by and disappeared behind a tent, loosing a cyclone in his belly.

Jake!

thirteen

Mason jumped to his feet, throwing the reins at Rebekah. He had to catch up with Jake before he disappeared again, or he might never find him again in this massive crowd. Mason stepped in front of Bekah, but she grabbed his sleeve, forcing him to stop.

Standing, she looked over her shoulder in the direction he stared. Mason offered a supporting hand against her back as the wagon jostled them down the road, moving in and out of dried ruts made by previous travelers. The wagon tilted to the side in a deep furrow. Mason grabbed Bekah's arm to keep her from tumbling over the side, all the while continuing to scan the crowded tent city, hoping to see Jake again.

"What is it?" Rebekah asked. Her voice sounded shakier than normal.

"I saw Jake. I've gotta catch up with him before he gets away."

She turned to face him, placing her hands against his chest for balance. "Think, Mason. You can't go chasing after Jake until we've set up camp; otherwise, you'll never find us in all the mess."

Mason clenched his teeth together, fighting his fierce desire to run after Jake and knowing her reasoning made sense. She and the children were his first priority. He focused his gaze on the Robinsons' wagon in front of him as it veered off the trail toward a small cluster of trees standing in a less crowded area of the tent city. Ella glared back at them, obviously wondering why they were standing while the wagon was still moving. For some reason Mason couldn't explain, he still didn't think Ella trusted him. Maybe it was because she'd become a mother hen to Bekah. He'd enjoyed Luther's company in the evenings, but at the same time, it meant less time with Bekah—although that was probably for the best since she'd be leaving soon.

He flopped down on the seat, biting back a grimace when his shoulder twinged with a brief spear of pain.

Think about finding Jake—not about saying good-bye to Bekah.

⁂

Rebekah sat down on the hard wagon seat next to Mason. She handed the reins to him, hoping he didn't notice her trembling. His sudden outburst had shaken her. In the weeks they'd traveled together, she hadn't seen him so intense and uneasy except maybe when she'd first met him. She couldn't understand why Mason was so intent on returning Jimmy and Katie to their father. After all, the man had abandoned them like Curtis had said her own father had left her. From what Mason had told her, Jake would be a complete stranger to Katie.

A pang of unexpected sympathy knotted her stomach. She leaned forward, elbows on her knees, and put her face in her hands. They smelled of leather and dust. How could she make Mason see that the children needed him to hang around, at least until they got used to Jake again?

Rebekah slid her hands over her ears. How would she ever sleep with the awful din of thousands of people roaring in her ears? Having grown up almost alone in the woods of Arkansas, rarely seeing anyone except her family, she felt the noise crowding in on her. She moved closer to Mason, but he didn't seem to notice.

He pulled the wagon to a stop beside the Robinsons' buckboard. "This looks like as good a place as any to camp," Luther hollered.

Rebekah's gaze traveled around the area, coming to rest on two tiny wooden structures, both with a long line of ragtag people winding away from them. The buildings were only about fifty feet from where the two wagons had stopped. This certainly wouldn't do.

She glanced past Mason to see Ella in an animated discussion with Luther. Ella's plump hands moved faster than a nervous cat trying to escape a room full of active children. Rebekah could just imagine the tongue-lashing Ella was giving him for suggesting camping so near the busy, aromatic outhouses.

Luther turned a frustrated gaze toward them. "Guess we'll be moseying on down the road a bit farther." He clicked his tired horses forward as Rebekah tightened her lips to hold back a grin.

"Don't know what's wrong with this campin' spot," Mason mumbled. "That Ella's just too picky."

Rebekah tried hard not to giggle, but a loud, unladylike snort broke loose. She couldn't hold back any longer. A loud laugh blasted past her lips. She leaned forward, forgetting her fear of the crowd, and enjoyed the feeling of amusement.

Mason peered down at her. "What's so funny?"

She shook her head as her whole body jiggled with laughter.

"What?" he asked with added emphasis.

Regaining control, Rebekah wiped the tears from her eyes. "I just imagined a glimpse of your face at dinner, trying to eat while sitting fifty feet downwind from the outhouses."

Mason's dark eyebrows crinkled in confusion. He pushed his hat up, revealing his pale forehead—an odd contrast to the rest of his tanned face. He looked back at the two little buildings, then turned to face her. His dark eyes glistened like the blue black of a crow's wing in the bright sunshine. "Oh," he said.

Rebekah turned her face away to keep from laughing at him. Men had such a different perspective on things. And Mason was all man; she couldn't deny that. Nor could she deny the way the closeness of him made her get all antsy inside. Their shoulders knocked together as they continued down the rutted road, giving her a sense of security and happiness like she'd never felt around any other man. Thoughts of her stepfather doused the joy in her spirit, sending her mirth fleeing as a pang of regret flooded through her. Her smile vanished, and once again she thought about leaving.

She scanned the crowd of people. Would she be safe from Curtis here? Was he even following her? And if he was, could he find her in this crowd? Children raced about, playing tag and squealing to one another. Jimmy shouted out the rear of the wagon at some boys as they galloped past, whooping like Indians. Tired women hung up faded clothing that looked even more worn out than their owners.

Rebekah shook her head; she didn't understand it. What could make so many people leave their homes, come to this horrid place, and live in such squalor, just for a chance at a small farm? She had a feeling most of them would leave empty-handed and disappointed. There couldn't possibly be enough land for all of them.

A nearby train whistle startled the horses. They snorted and whinnied and pranced sideways in their harnesses. Mason had to grip the reins to keep them from bolting. His arm, muscles tight, pressed against hers. He muttered soothing words to his team. She glanced down, realizing just how close she sat to him. She had to start distancing herself from Mason and the children, or she'd be suffering the pain of separation for a long time.

Rebekah slid over to the far side of the wagon seat, wondering how much a train ticket to Wichita, Kansas, would cost. She'd counted her little pile of coins a few days ago. The money she'd made back home from selling eggs and the fowl she'd hunted was pitifully meager. She calculated the amount again. Would it be enough? She could only pray it would.

Luther eased off the trail to an area that looked large enough for both wagons. He set the brake and hopped down before Ella could comment on the spot he'd selected. Mason pulled alongside, leaving about ten feet between the wagons. They could set up their campfire in the middle, giving their little group a bit of privacy.

Rebekah stretched, wishing she could take a nap like Katie had earlier. With her thoughts on leaving and never seeing Mason again, sleep had been hard to come by lately. She hoped Mason could find Jake quickly so she'd be free to leave. No sense in postponing the inevitable.

She shook her head. It was best not to think on those things. Wasn't there a verse in the Bible that said to think on good things? Tonight, after dinner, she'd try to find it.

Good things. Denver. Jimmy and Katie seeing their dad again. At least she hoped that was good. Mason's smile—no, that didn't count. A home of her own. Children someday. A vision of Jimmy and Katie chasing butterflies in a field with her watching from the porch swing of her own little home and Mason sitting next to her flittered across Rebekah's mind. Ohhh! Thinking good thoughts was harder than she had imagined.

She didn't even notice Mason had climbed off the wagon until he reached up to help her down, pulling her from her mental battle. *Don't think so far ahead—maybe that's the key.* Dinner. Setting up camp. She reached out, holding on to Mason's broad shoulders as he lifted her down. She noticed his lips were pursed into a tight line.

"What's the matter?"

"Nothin'. Lots of things." He released her and reached up to adjust his hat. "I've gotta find Jake, but I need to get you all settled first."

"We can set up camp if you want to start searching," she offered.

A spark flickered in his eyes then quickly faded. He looked up at the sky and shook his head. "It'll be dark before too long. We need to get supper and get the kids bedded down."

"All right. I'll get the food started." She looked around. "I guess it's a good thing we gathered up some firewood this morning. I don't know what we'll do when we run out, what with all these folks around here needing wood, too." Mason's gaze drifted away from her face and focused somewhere behind her.

"Howdy, neighbors."

Rebekah turned to see a tall, thin man walking toward them. His worn overalls were covered in multicolored patches, and some of the patches had patches. She looked down to his bare feet, filthy dirty from who-knew-how-many days of walking.

"My name's Homer Banning. You reckon you and your missus could spare some water?"

"I—" Rebekah slammed her mouth shut when Mason squeezed her shoulder. She wanted to set this man straight right off. He needed to know she wasn't Mason's wife, but with Mason's arm hanging lightly around her shoulders, she couldn't think straight.

"I see that you folks just rode in, so's I figured you must have some fresh water," Mr. Banning said.

"Sure—" Mason's grip tightened on her shoulder, cutting off her words again. He pulled her close to his side, sabotaging her brain.

"I'd like to be hospitable, but we don't have any water to spare. Sorry."

"I'm willing to pay—a nickel a cup." Mr. Banning reached in his pocket and pulled out a handful of coins. "Some folks is charging up ta fifteen cents a cup, but I cain't pay that much. Ten's more reasonable."

Horrified, Rebekah gaped at the sea of humanity. People were actually buying water? She'd never heard of such a thing. Surely they could spare a bit of water. Mr. Banning didn't look like he had a nickel to spare. She turned to face Mason and leaned in close. "Surely we can spare a little water," she whispered.

Mason glared at her with that look he'd used when she'd first tried to leave his camp. "No."

"But—"

"I said no, Bekah." Mason looked past her and scowled. "See why." He gently turned her around. A group of six or seven people headed toward them. Rebekah took a step back until she could feel her back touching Mason's chest. Surely all these folks didn't need water.

"I'm real sorry, Mr. Banning, but we've got two kids to care for and four horses. We need all the water we've got." Mason's voice tickled her ear. She loved his smooth Southern accent. When he said "I'm," it sounded more like "ah'm."

"Now see here, you've got two barrels. All I want is a canteen full." Homer Banning moved forward just as Jimmy popped his head out of the front of the wagon.

"Got my boots on. Can I get down?" he asked.

"Back inside, now!" Mason snarled. Rebekah glanced up in time to see Jimmy's shocked expression, but the boy didn't argue. He simply disappeared inside. She heard Katie's little voice talking to Jimmy. He shushed her quiet, obviously hoping to hear what was going on outside.

Mason moved around, then stepped in front of her, rifle in hand. "I don't want any trouble," he said. "I'm just looking out for my own." She peeked around him so she could see Mr. Banning. "There's a whole river full of water half a mile away."

Mr. Banning looked at the rifle and scowled. She wondered if the thought of going the half-mile to the river was so much of an effort for him that he'd risk getting shot. He glared at Mason again then turned and stomped off. The small crowd of people gathered around Mr. Banning. "He's not sharin'," she heard him mutter.

In unison, the group of people glanced at Mason. He straightened, raising his chin in the air as if daring them to approach him. After a moment, they turned away, looking tired and discouraged, and dispersed in different directions. Rebekah blew out the breath she'd been holding.

"I want Webekah," Katie cried through the canvas wagon top.

Mason pivoted around, nearly smacking Rebekah in the head with the rifle because she was so near. "I want you and the kids to stay real close to the wagon and the Robinsons until we know which way the wind's blowin' around here. Could be they were just testin' us to see how soft we are." He glanced over his shoulder, and seeming to feel the danger was past, he leaned over her and set the rifle on the wagon seat.

Rebekah closed her eyes, savoring his closeness as his chest brushed against her forehead. She suddenly saw Mason's wisdom in removing his sling. Would those people have forced the issue if he had faced them one-armed? She didn't even seem to mind that he was bossing her around again.

"Thanks for backing me up, Luther." Mason looked past her, and Rebekah peeked over her shoulder to see Luther walking around the front of the horses, back toward his wagon. She hadn't realized he'd been there to support them. Warmth flooded her. It felt good to have friends watching out for her. That was something she'd never had before.

"Bekah." Mason grasped her chin and turned her face toward him. "I'm serious. Stay close tomorrow while I'm gone."

She tilted her head back and glanced up at him. By the tone of his voice, she could almost convince herself that he cared for her. "You're not going looking for Jake tonight?"

He removed his hat, ran his hands through his hair, then blew out a breath that warmed her cheek. "No. I don't think I can risk leaving you and the kids after what just happened." He rolled the edges of his hat then slapped it back on.

Rebekah's spine tingled with excitement as she stared up at his stubbly chin. He wanted to protect her *and* the children. Maybe he really did care—at least a little.

"I don't want to lose the water. Did you see that water in the river? It was almost yellow."

The water. Her excitement plummeted down and mixed with the dust at her feet. She should have known he was concerned for the water, not her.

"Tomorrow I'll start looking for Jake. That is, as long as we don't have any more trouble." Mason walked to the back of the wagon. "C'mon out, kiddos."

Tomorrow. Tomorrow she'd find out how much train fare to Denver was.

fourteen

Rebekah yawned and stretched, not quite ready for dawn. Half the night, she'd tossed and turned, trying to erase the pain of Mason being more concerned about the water than about her. She didn't know why she expected more when no man had *ever* cared for her. Her real father died. Her stepfather was willing to trade her to his old drinking buddy for a few bottles of moonshine and half a side of beef.

Was there something wrong with her? Rebekah shook her head. No, she wouldn't believe that. Her mother had told her that God loves everyone and that each person is special in their own way. There must be some way that she was special.

Sitting up, she rubbed the sleep from her eyes then peeked at Katie. The toddler lay on her side with her thumb halfway in her mouth. Tears blurred Rebekah's eyes at the thought of never seeing her sweet smile again. At least Ella had softened her stance on what was respectable and allowed her to sleep in the wagon with Katie.

It would be good for the children to have a real home again. Maybe Jake would get a piece of land in the Run and settle down with the kids. Then she could write to them—if Jake would allow it.

Ignoring the chill in the air, she quickly dressed in the early morning light. Crawling out the back of the wagon, she looked for Mason. She'd heard him walking around outside the wagon until she finally drifted off to sleep. Must have been protecting his precious water.

Rebekah wanted to slap herself for her bad attitude. Come the heat of the day, she'd be thankful for that water. She couldn't help feeling sorry for all the other people who were running low, but Mason was right: If they started handing out water, it would be gone in no time.

Mason must have been up half the night, because he was still curled up beside Jimmy next to the cold campfire. He rarely slept past dawn. Against her will, Rebekah studied him. She seldom had the luxury of staring at his hair, since it was usually hidden under his big Western hat. Now the ebony locks fell across his forehead, giving him a youthful look. Dark stubble shadowed his firm jaw. Deep breaths of sleep blew across lips that were wonderful to kiss.

She blinked back her tears, knowing she'd never kiss them again. Rebekah turned abruptly. She had to find something to occupy her thoughts, or she'd stumble into the quagmire of self-pity and be stuck for good.

"You ever gonna tell him how you feel?"

Rebekah jumped. She looked up, surprised to see Ella sitting on the tailgate of her buckboard. "I. . .uh, what do you mean?" She rubbed her eyes, hoping Ella would think she was clearing the sleep from them rather than tears.

"You're crazy in love with Mason. It's written all over your face." Ella pulled her foot up onto her knee and began lacing her shoes.

Rebekah's hands flew up to touch her cheeks. Did she love Mason? Was that what she was feeling? And was it obvious to everyone else? She glanced around to see if any of their close neighbors were listening. Thankfully, nobody nearby was stirring yet.

"Now don't go fretting on me. I doubt he knows. Men are slow on the uptake 'bout things of the heart."

She moved over closer to Ella. If the older woman kept talking so loudly, everyone in the camp, including Mason, would know how she felt. She was thankful Luther was nowhere in sight. He wasn't the type to keep information to himself.

"You gotta plain tell a man. Don't 'spect him to figure it out on his own."

"It doesn't matter anyway." Rebekah peeked at Ella then glanced back down at her laced fingers. "Mason doesn't love me; he still loves his dead wife."

Ella slipped off the wagon and came to stand in front of her. The older woman took Rebekah's hands in hers. "I don't know as I believe that. I've seen how he looks at you. That man's just full of hurt and anger at God. Till he gets that out of his system, he don't have room to love someone else."

Rebekah absorbed Ella's words. There was wisdom in what she said. The only problem was that by the time Mason got over his hurt, he'd be out west and she'd be in Denver. At least she could pray for Mason to find peace with God. Knowing he did would make her happy.

"Thank you, Ella." Rebekah pulled Ella into her arms. She appreciated having a woman to talk to and share things with. "Will you write to me in Denver?"

Ella pushed away. "Denver. Hmpff!" She turned back to her wagon and began pulling out cooking supplies. "Best get that notion out of that pretty little head of yours," she mumbled.

Rebekah smiled. It felt good to know someone would miss her after she was gone. She turned back to her own wagon—Mason's wagon—and began hunting for something to cook for breakfast.

※

Mason wandered from tent to tent looking for Jake. He'd started in the area where he'd seen the man the day before and was now working his way back toward the Conestoga. The sound of hammers echoed behind him. Today he'd witnessed the birth of a town as people began erecting buildings that would make this more than just a tent city. Bekah's delicious pancakes warmed his belly while thoughts of her warmed his heart. Just as quickly those thoughts grew cold.

Things had been so much easier before she came. No, that wasn't true. Not easier—less complicated. Bekah's help had been invaluable. Now he wondered how he'd managed to cook and care for the kids and handle everything else without her help.

But he'd been focused then. Give the kids back to Jake and head west. Simple. He yanked off his hat and rubbed his forehead with his palm. Why did women always have to mess up a perfectly good plan? He didn't like his mind being all frazzled, useless like an old frayed rope. A man needed a plan. He needed to think clearly—and women had a way of fogging up a man's mind.

"Well, well, if it ain't that no-good brother-in-law of mine."

Mason slapped his hat back on as he spun around at the sound of the familiar voice. Jake stood there, dressed in nearly new black pants and a fancy pale blue shirt with frills on the front. He looked like a dandy—a gambler. Mason narrowed his eyes. He could handle his brother-in-law's restlessness and inability to settle down, but to find out he was a low-down gambler sparked Mason's short fuse. He clenched his teeth together to keep from saying something he'd regret.

"Whoa, now." Jake raised his hands in defense. "That's not a very friendly welcome for a relative."

Mason fought the urge to plow his fist through that big, toothy grin of Jake's. "We're no longer relatives—or did you not get my telegram?" The man finally had the decency to look chagrined, and his smile faded.

"Yeah, I got it."

"And you couldn't see your way clear to come home and visit your wife's grave?"

Jake pulled off his bowler hat and fiddled with the short brim. "I didn't get the message until about a month afterwards. By then it was too late to do anything about it."

Mason ground his teeth together. "And what about your kids? Did you think even once about them and what they were going through losing their mother after they'd already lost their father?"

"They didn't lose their father," Jake ground out defensively. "I've been working—trying to make some money for 'em."

Mason noticed people staring as they walked by, giving a wide berth around them. He turned his gaze back on Jake and lowered his voice. "And just what do you think would have happened to Jimmy and Katie if I hadn't been around to care for them?"

Jake shrugged. "I knew you would, so I didn't worry."

"Do you have any idea how hard it is to run two farms and care for two young children? They aren't my responsibility—they're yours." As soon as he said the words, a sharp pain gutted him. It sounded almost like he didn't care for his niece and nephew.

"So did you sell my farm?"

Mason balled up his fist in his effort not to slug Jake. Was money all he cared about? "Yep, I sold it. Mine, too. How else could I get the money to bring the kids out here?"

"Jimmy and Katie are here?" Jake looked around. "Where?"

"Back at camp," Mason grumbled.

"Well, let's go see 'em. They'll be happy to see their ol' man." Jake set his hat back on his slicked-down hair; then he grinned.

"What are you grinnin' about?"

"Just trying to imagine you changing Katie's diapers."

Mason straightened. "Katie doesn't wear diapers anymore—hasn't for a long time."

Confusion flickered in Jake's eyes. "Guess they've grown some, huh?"

"Kids grow a lot in two years." Mason started for camp. The last thing he wanted to do was take Jake to see the kids, but this was the whole reason he'd made the trip, wasn't it? Jake walked along beside him with a slight limp Mason didn't remember. His brother-in-law was thinner and looked older than his thirty years.

Moving around a group of children playing ring-around-the-rosy, Mason watched Jake from the corner of his eye as they walked toward camp. "So you been gamblin'?" Jake wore a poker face if Mason ever saw one.

"Uhh. . .yeah. I've made a nice little nest egg. I'm planning on racing in the Run and getting me some land. I've already scoped out a nice little quarter section." Jake smiled his first natural smile. "You should see it, Mase. Prettiest section of rolling green hills with a creek flowing through it."

Mason stopped and turned to face Jake. "You're one of those Sooners—those folks who've snuck in and tried to stake a claim before the Run?" He couldn't believe it—on second thought, it sounded just like Jake.

"Pretty smart, huh?" Jake straightened his lapels then tucked in his fancy shirt.

"Pretty dumb. The army's shootin' Sooners."

"Well, they are now, but they weren't last month." Jake tipped his hat at two teenage girls who giggled and snickered as they walked by. "Nice." He whistled through his teeth.

Mason wanted to be sick. Jake was making eyes at schoolgirls. What had Danielle ever seen in him? Jake had never been any good, as far as he was concerned. Suddenly Mason stopped dead in his tracks. How could he honestly turn Jimmy and Katie over to a no-good like Jake Conners?

"What is it?" Jake stopped, too, and looked at the people passing around them.

The cadence of voices buzzed in Mason's ears. The reality of his plan slapped him full in the face for the first time. There was no way he could give the children to Jake. The man would never take care of them or protect them.

"C'mon, Mase. I wanna see my kids."

Mason's first thought was to turn around and lose Jake in the throng of the crowd. It wouldn't take much effort. Then he could pack up Rebekah and the kids and head out. But to where? He had enough money to buy a little farm somewhere, but his plan had been to head west, and he didn't have enough money to get four people halfway across the country and still have enough to start over.

Who was he kidding anyway? The children didn't belong to him. Rebekah didn't belong to him. In fact, almost half the money he had hidden in the bottom of his wagon belonged to Jake and the kids.

"What is wrong with you?"

Mason stared at Jake. How could he explain his feelings to this man when he didn't understand them himself?

"Uncle Mason!" Jimmy's call broke into his thoughts. He hadn't realized they were at camp already. "Where ya been all day?"

"I. . .uh. . ."

"Jimmy, boy, have you ever grown!" Jake looked at his son like any proud papa would.

"Do I know you?" Jimmy's gaze focused on Jake's face; then his boyish features registered alarm, and he glanced at Mason. Suddenly he took a step back, almost knocking down Katie. "Pa?"

Jake slapped his thigh and cackled. "That's right, son. I'm your pa."

Worry crinkled Jimmy's forehead. Katie's features resembled her brother's. She stepped around him and surveyed Jake, looking him up and down. Katie crossed her pudgy arms across her chest and tapped her toe.

"Nuh-uh, you ain't our pa. Unca Mathon is."

fifteen

Jake whirled around, and his usual congenial countenance sparked into something almost vicious. "You told Katie you were her pa?"

Mason stood speechless. He'd never so much as insinuated such a thing. He shook his head, noticing a blur of skirt and blond hair as Katie rushed over and grabbed him around the leg.

"He's not my pa. You're my pa!" Katie screamed into his thigh.

Jake reached out and tugged on her arm. "Katie, I'm your pa. Don't you recognize me?"

She turned her head away and tightened her grip on Mason's leg. "Nooo! You's not my pa."

Mason reached down and patted her head, pressing it against his leg. "Shhh, sugar, it'll be okay."

Jake tugged on Katie's arm again. The little girl let out a bloodcurdling scream.

Holding up her skirt, Rebekah raced around the side of the wagon, her blue eyes wide with concern. "Katie—"

She halted so fast, her long braid flopped over her shoulder and slapped her across the chest. She looked from Katie to Mason to Jake. "Is everything okay? What's going on?"

"Webekahhh!" Katie cried as she suddenly released Mason and ran to Rebekah. Bekah stooped down, opening her arms, and Katie hurried into her embrace. "Tell him Unca Mathon is my pa."

"Oh, sweetie, it's okay." Rebekah stood and hugged Katie, her questioning gaze locked with Mason's.

After a moment of drawing strength from Rebekah's stare, Mason broke his gaze free. He realized they were drawing a crowd. Jake paced back and forth, looking like a polecat that had eaten some rank meat. Jimmy watched his dad with wide eyes. Luther, armed with his old shotgun, stood next to Ella.

"Show's over, folks. You'd best just tend to your own business," Mason said to the crowd. He placed his hands on his hips and glared until people slowly began to disperse and the buzz of speculation faded.

"You're the last person I'd expect to shoot me in the back like this, Mase." Jake stood in a stance similar to Mason's, glaring through his pale blue eyes. The words gutted Mason worse than the point of a brand-new bowie knife.

"Let's take this to the privacy of our camp." With a wave of his hand, Mason motioned the direction to Jake. Jimmy raced off ahead of them, while Rebekah carried Katie. Katie wrapped her arms around Bekah's neck and her legs around Bekah's waist.

In silence, they walked together to the campsite. Blocked by the wagons on two sides and grazing horses on the third, they had a fair amount of privacy. They gathered in a rough circle, and Mason opened his mouth to speak. In that instant, he heard the *click* of a rifle being cocked.

Jimmy stood on the wagon seat, looking like a fierce soldier, the rifle pointed straight at Jake. "You ain't takin' my sister," he glowered.

Mason heard Rebekah's gasp as he moved toward Jimmy. "Now just hold on there, pardner. No call to get all fired up." Jimmy eyed him with a mixture of defiance and uncertainty. "Give me the rifle and hop down. We'll get this all worked out, okay?"

Rubbing the back of his neck, Mason watched the different expressions cross Jimmy's face as the boy decided what to do. Mason felt certain Jimmy wouldn't shoot his own father. The boy could barely shoot a duck for dinner.

For the first time, Mason considered how his leaving might affect the children. In his mind, he'd been planning this ever since Danielle's death; but to the kids, finding their father had been an adventure until the reality of their separation with him set in. He'd never once thought how hard that might be on them. His leaving would be another loss they'd have to suffer.

"Jimmy," Rebekah's firm but gentle voice called softly beside Mason. The boy looked from his father to her. "Please, Jimmy, give Mason the rifle. I know you don't want to hurt your father." Defiance flickered in his nephew's dark gaze. "What if you missed and hit me—or Katie?" Instantly Jimmy wilted and lowered the rifle. Mason blew out a deep breath he just realized he'd been holding, then snagged the weapon out of Jimmy's hands, tossing it into the back of the wagon. He pulled Jimmy off the wagon seat and wrapped his arms around the boy.

Like two parents ready to do battle for their children, Mason and Rebekah stood side by side, each holding a child. Jake whirled to face Bekah, fury blazing across his lean features. "Just who are you to be telling my boy what to do?"

"Don't yell at Webekah," Katie cried.

Mason cast a glance at Ella, beseeching her with his eyes for help. The older woman immediately picked up his signal. "Luther and me had a hankering to take a walk about town and see them new buildings they're tossing up. Jimmy, you and Katie come on along with us and give the grown-ups here a chance to yammer some."

"You won't leave?" Jimmy asked Mason. His eyes reminded Mason of a skittish mustang.

"No, pard, I'm not going anywhere." He gave his nephew a hug then set him on the ground. For the first time in months, Mason had a feeling he might not be heading west after all.

Katie took a little longer to be convinced to leave Bekah's arms, but finally the Robinsons and the children walked out of camp.

"Why don't we all sit down and have some coffee?" Rebekah gave a little half smile then turned without waiting for a response.

Mason could sense her apprehension. He shook his head.

Never once had he considered the children wouldn't want to go with their father. Mason and Jake sat down on a couple of large rocks and waited for Bekah's return.

"You wanna tell me what's goin' on and who this woman is, Masc?" Jake's tone had softened somewhat. Evidently, having his own son point a rifle at him had shaken him up, too.

"Her name is Rebekah," Mason said. Bekah disappeared in the wagon, looking for tin cups, he guessed.

"Yeah, but who is she? You and her ain't married, are you?"

"No." Mason shook his head, knowing a part of him deep inside wished he could answer yes.

Jake's eyes flashed and his nostrils flared. "She's not a—you know, a loose woman, is she?"

Mason jumped to his feet, ready to pommel Jake's face into mashed potatoes. How could he think that about her? *God, I could use some help here.* Unclenching his fist, Mason realized he'd just uttered his first proper prayer in half a year. He heard the clinking of metal behind him then felt Bekah's soft touch in the small of his back.

"Let it go," she whispered. "It's not important." She stepped around him, trailing her arm along his waistline, sending tingling sparks shooting up his spine. The fingers of her other hand were looped through the handles of three blue tin mugs, making her fist look like some kind of strange club. She held her right hand out to Jake and smiled. "I'm Rebekah Bailey, and your brother-in-law saved my life."

Jake's mouth fell open, and he halfheartedly shook Bekah's hand. Mason felt pride surge through him that she'd be more concerned with his pride than her own.

For the next half hour, they sat talking and drinking their coffee. Rebekah shared how they'd met. Mason told Jake how much help she'd been caring for him and the kids, especially after he'd been injured. Bekah blushed and all but hid behind her coffee cup. He told Jake of his quest to locate him so he could return the kids and then go west. Bekah's gaze darkened and she took on a faraway look.

All too soon, the children returned with the Robinsons. Jimmy and Katie squeezed in between Mason and Bekah. Neither seemed excited at all to see their father; in fact, they were just the opposite.

"I can't believe how much you two have grown," Jake said. "Jimmy, you'd just turned five last time I was home, and you, Katie, were still a baby."

"I'm not a baby," Katie said, a little louder than necessary. "I'm fwee."

"Well, three's still little." Jake gave her a wry smile.

"Nuh-uh. I'm a big girwl."

Mason knew he should scold Katie for talking to Jake so, but he didn't have the heart.

"Katie," Bekah said, "it isn't nice to talk to your father like that."

Great! Bekah's braver than me. But then he already knew that. Hadn't she boldly faced him every time he'd tried to get her to do something she didn't want to? She wasn't one to back down—though she did have a problem with running away at times.

Mason tore his gaze away from Bekah and realized Katie was crying.

"C'mon, sweetie," Bekah said. "I think you're ready for your nap."

Bekah picked up Katie and took her inside the wagon. The Robinsons were nowhere to be found. Jimmy had finally warmed a bit and was talking with Jake. Watching them, Mason knew his life was fixing to change in a big way, but he didn't know if he was ready to handle that change. He suddenly realized that it had been days since he'd thought of Annie—maybe even a week. It was one thing to lose a woman to death, but totally another thing to lose one because she wanted something more than she wanted him. Mason looked heavenward. *God, I think I may need Your help with this.*

❧

Now that Katie had fallen asleep and the men were still

talking, Rebekah finally had a chance to slip away and check on the price of her train ticket. She'd counted her money last night and hoped her measly amount would be enough.

Please, God, make it be.

She slipped out of the back of the wagon and headed for the depot. Soon she spotted the brand-new pine building that housed the ticket booth and waiting area. As she approached the building, the smell of freshly cut pine mixed with the pungent aroma of coal. The new platform was already darkened from coal dust and the shoes of travelers hoping for a new start. A few hundred feet from the depot, the train tracks ended.

Rebekah hopped up the three steps to the platform just as the train chugged and spewed backward out of the depot. She raised her hand to her mouth to keep from inhaling the black smoke and coal dust. Her insides quivered. What would it be like to journey in the belly of such a beast and to travel so fast? Shaking off her apprehension, she looked around the depot. Some of the people who'd recently arrived still wandered about with the same dazed expression she knew must have been on her face the first time she saw the enormous tent city and the myriad of people, all vying for the same land.

The arrival times posted next to the ticket cage indicated three trains per day arriving every day except Sunday. With the Land Run only fours days away, the population in the area could easily double if each of the trains was full. Where would all these people live and find water?

Rebekah stepped up to the counter and waited until the clerk turned around and noticed her. He wore what she figured was the typical train clerk garb—black pants and white shirt, with a flat black cap and string tie.

"Howdy, ma'am. What can I do for you?" He laced his slender fingers and gave her a businesslike smile, reminding her of a fox she once nursed after it had gotten caught in one of Curtis's traps.

"Can I get a ticket to Denver?"

"You betcha." He rubbed his pale hand over his jaw. "Course, you'll have to switch trains a couple of times. Be best to go to Wichita first and overnight there."

"Okay, then, I'll take a ticket to Wichita." Rebekah fingered the coins in her pocket, praying they'd be enough. She'd worry about what she'd do next when she got to Wichita.

"You'll pert near have the whole train to yourself, I reckon. Folks these days are wantin' to come *into* the Territories, not leave." He cackled like he'd told the funniest joke in the world. When she didn't laugh, he sniffed then looked down into a book filled with prices.

He quoted the price. *Two dollars and twenty-five cents!* That was almost twice the money she had. Rebekah thanked the man and headed back to camp. How could she earn the money she needed in such a short time? The last thing she wanted was to be stranded here or live with the Robinsons, as Ella had suggested. With the kids back with Jake soon, she knew she couldn't travel with Mason any longer.

Rebekah fought against the tears blurring her vision. She wouldn't cry—not here where so many people could see. Holding her head up, she ignored the stares and whistles of the men she passed.

Please, God. Show me a way to make the money I need. You helped me get away from Curtis and sent Mason to help me and protect me. Now I'm asking You to show me a way to make some money.

Walking back to camp, she decided to make a stop at the ever-busy outhouse. The bright afternoon sun had nipped the chill out of the spring day, making her crave a drink of Mason's water. As she waited her turn in the long line of women, she studied the men in the nearby line to their outhouse. They ranged from young boys to old, bent seniors; some dressed in fancy city clothes while others sported faded overalls.

After about ten minutes of waiting, her ears honed in on a particular voice. "Lookie here," said a middle-aged man dressed in a flannel shirt and black pants. "I only got one button left on this here shirt. There ain't no general store here so's I can buy some new ones, and even if I did, I don't know nuthin' 'bout how to fasten them on." He heaved a sigh.

"Just look at all those women." The tall, thin man standing next to him waved his hand in the air, pointing at the line of ladies. "Can't you get one of them to hook them buttons onto your shirt?"

The other man looked up and down the line then shrugged. "You know I don't know any of them womenfolk. Their menfolk might not take kindly to me askin' one of 'em to take up clothes fixin' fer me."

"You could pay her."

A lady with a young girl exited the privy. Rebekah stepped forward with the other women, her mind buzzing with ideas, and formulated a plan. Suddenly she swirled around to the woman standing behind her. "Would you hold my place in line for a moment, please?" The woman nodded, eyeing her skeptically.

Rebekah took a deep breath, hoping to steady her wobbly knees, and started forward. "Uh. . .excuse me, sir, I don't mean to be eavesdropping, but I just happened to hear your conversation." The two men glanced at one another, then broke into grins like children at Christmas. Rebekah wondered if it was because a female had had the nerve to approach them. "I can sew buttons on your shirt. Uh. . .I mean for ten cents each—and I'll supply the buttons. Course, they might not all match."

The men exchanged glances again; then the buttonless man looked down and counted the buttonholes on his shirt. "That'd be forty cents. Why, I can pert near buy a whole shirt for that."

"Not in this town, you can't." Rebekah held her ground, knowing she'd just come upon an idea that could easily earn her the money she needed.

"Twenty-five cents," he countered.

Rebekah straightened. Thrusting her chin in the air, she

turned her back to the man and started to walk away. "Oh, all right, how about thirty cents for this shirt, and I'll pay you to fix my other shirt, too?"

She knew she must be grinning like a possum as she spun back around. Maybe watching Curtis barter so many times had taught her a thing or two. "Done!"

"My name's Ben Hopper, and this here's my sister's boy, Carl." Ben undid the single button on his shirt and started to shed it right there.

Rebekah glanced around, noticing for the first time all the people watching them and how the buzz of voices near them had quieted. Most of the faces were filled with curiosity and a few with disapproval. "Uh. . .wait, Ben." She raised her hand to halt his undressing. "I'm gonna have to go back to my wagon and fetch my box of buttons and sewing supplies. Why don't we meet under that big tree in about half an hour?" She pointed across the field to one of the few trees offering shade to the weary bunch of travelers.

"All righty. I'll do it, and I thank ya kindly." Ben stuck out a not-too-clean-looking hand. Hesitantly, Rebekah reached forward with her fingertips and gave it a little shake. She had just started her own little business. She raised her head, proud of her accomplishment. "Oh, by the way, my name is Rebekah. And please tell your friends I'd be happy to sew buttons or do repairs on their shirts, too."

The men tipped their worn hats and mumbled, "Pleased to meet'cha," in unison. Rebekah smiled then returned to her place in line, thanking God for answering her prayer so quickly.

From behind her she heard someone mumble, "Ain't proper-like for a young woman to be mending clothes for total strangers."

Rebekah cringed at the rude comment but refused to turn around to look at her accuser. That person had no idea how desperate she was. If she didn't find a way to earn some money, she could soon find herself living alone without home or friends. Maybe it wasn't exactly proper, but if she stayed in plain view of everyone, surely she and her reputation would be safe.

She felt certain God had arranged this opportunity for her. If only she could be sure Mason would feel the same way. If he opposed the idea, he would try to stop her. Maybe she wouldn't tell him. He wasn't her boss. After all, he cared more for a barrel of water than he did for her.

Rebekah began calculating how many buttons she'd have to sew on in order to have enough money to buy her ticket. If she were lucky, she might make enough to get her all the way to Denver without having to stay and find work in Wichita. It felt good to focus on her goal. She wouldn't think about how much leaving Mason and the kids would hurt. But she was happy to have met them and to have had a glimpse at what it felt like to be part of a loving family. Mason didn't think of himself as father material, but she had a feeling he was a much better father to Jimmy and Katie than Jake would ever be. If only there were a way Mason could keep the children. . .and her. But then, he didn't even want her.

Back at their camp, Rebekah climbed into the rear of the wagon. She peeked at Katie, thankful the little girl was still asleep. She folded a pile of clothing and picked up the toys Katie had played with earlier, then located her carpetbag. Inside was a small tin can filled with her mother's button collection, several spools of thread, and a couple of needles. When she ran away from Curtis, she'd wondered why she'd felt such a strong inclination to take her mother's button box; now she knew it had been God's prompting. God's provision.

Holding the tin steady so it wouldn't rattle, she climbed out of the wagon. Mason, Jake, and Jimmy still sat around the campfire, talking and reminiscing. As she approached they stood, though Jake rose a bit more slowly than Mason and Jimmy, almost as if it were an afterthought. Mason greeted her with a reserved smile.

"I don't mean to disturb you all," she said, glancing from

Mason to Jake and Jimmy. "But if you're going to be here talking for a while, I thought I'd go help some folks for a bit."

"What folks?" Mason said as he approached her.

Rebekah shrugged. "Just some people I met—who need some help."

"I don't think it's a good idea for you to go running around here unescorted." Mason waved his hand in the air. "There's a whole passel of unsavory people here."

"Aw, let her alone, Mase." Jake strode over and stood next to Mason. " 'Sides, you don't own her. She's got a right to go wherever she wants."

Mason scowled at Jake then skewered Rebekah with his glare. She lifted her chin and met his gaze evenly, though her heart raced faster than a mustang on the run. Jake was right; Mason wasn't in charge of her. Still, she didn't want to displease him. He'd been good to her, but she had no choice. She had to make the money she needed, even if Mason didn't like her traipsing about on her own.

"There's nothing to worry about," she said. "I've been walking about for more than an hour, and nobody has bothered me. In fact, most folks are friendly."

Mason crossed his arms, stared down at her for a moment, then turned back toward the camp. "Guess you'll be on your own soon enough," he mumbled.

"I've been on my own for a while now," she said as she turned and walked away from camp.

sixteen

"No, Jake. I'm not riding in the Land Run, and that's final!" Mason wasn't about to be sucked into one of Jake's schemes.

"Now listen to me, Mase." Jake glanced around and moved in closer to him. "I've seen the land," he whispered. "I've been there already."

Mason narrowed his eyes, struggling to grasp Jake's meaning.

"I've found the most beautiful quarter section of land. Rolling green hills. A creek that cuts across the top third of the land. A section of trees just begging for a house to throw shade on."

Mason had seen that faraway look in Jake's eyes before. It was the same look he got every time he birthed another one of his harebrained ideas that took him from his family. He shook his head, unsure of what land Jake was referring to.

Jake's eye sparked with excitement. "It's perfect, I tell ya, and it's gonna be mine."

"What's going to be yours?"

"Aren't you listening? I told you I've been in the Unassigned Lands."

Mason blinked, remembering what Jake had said the day they'd found him. "I still find it hard to believe you're one of those Sooners."

"Boomer. Sooner. Lots of folks got different names for it, but, yeah, I'm one of them."

"That's just plum crazy, Jake. The soldiers are arresting and even shooting Sooners." Mason thrust his hands on his hips. "You're just beggin' for trouble, aren't you?"

Jake curled his lip but didn't respond. He squatted by the campfire and poured himself a cup of coffee. The fresh scent tickled Mason's nose. He stooped beside his brother-in-law,

143

helping himself after Jake set the coffeepot back on the fire. He swirled the black liquid around, listening to the sounds of people all around. Children squealed; a baby cried. Dogs barked; horses whinnied. Life went on all around him. A smile crept to his lips when he saw Jimmy lasso one of his friends across the way. Every so often, he'd hear Katie or Bekah's soft chatter in the wagon.

What if he went west and something happened to Jake? What would become of the children then? How could he just get on his horse and ride away? Maybe if Jake married again—but where would he find someone willing to marry a homeless vagabond with two children?

Rebekah's laugh drew his gaze toward the wagon. Hoisting her skirt, she climbed backward out over the tailgate. Katie's chubby arms emerged from behind the yellowing canvas, and Bekah lifted her out of the wagon. "My, but you're getting big," she said. Katie giggled, giving Rebekah a tight hug around the neck before being set on the ground.

Rebekah turned her head, smiling when her gaze caught Mason's. Somewhere in his belly, he felt a zing of emotion. "Katie and I are going for a little walk." She smiled and gave a wave. She and Katie had been going on lots of little walks in the past few days. Bekah's arms held several articles of clothing he didn't recognize. He wasn't sure, but he had a feeling Bekah was working on her own scheme of some sort. She and Jake would make quite a pair. *Whoa!* Where had that thought come from—and more importantly, how did he feel about it?

Her long braid swung like the pendulum of a mantel clock, ticktocking back and forth. Katie skipped along beside her. Anyone who didn't know them would surely think they were mother and daughter. Mason peeked over at Jake. Bekah needed a home. Jake needed a wife. The kids loved her. It seemed like a perfect solution. He could ride west and no longer have to worry about the children—Bekah would take care of them. But who would take care of her? He sure couldn't count on Jake for that. *Bekah deserves better than Jake*, he thought, pushing away the feelings of unrest and jealousy that surfaced at the thought of Bekah and Jake together. Still. . .it would solve his problem.

"Why you scowlin'? I don't think you heard a word I said." Jake tossed his coffee grounds into the fire. The flame flared and sizzled, filling the air with the pungent scent of burnt coffee.

"I heard you."

"So what do ya think? Will you ride with me and try to get the land next to mine?" Jake pinned him with a hopeful stare.

Okay, so maybe he hadn't been listening all that closely. He didn't want the land next to Jake's. His heart couldn't handle seeing Rebekah with Jake. That would be worse than watching her get on the train and head for Denver. When had he started to care about her so much?

"Mason. Pay attention. This is important." He looked up to see Jake staring at him. "If we both ride, we'll have a double chance of getting the land I want. If something happens to me, you can claim it."

For once, what Jake said made sense, but Mason shook his head. "It's too late. The Run's tomorrow and I haven't registered."

Jake broke out in a smile that would rival a kid's at Christmas. "Not a problem." He strode over to where his saddle lay next to the wagon. For several moments, Jake rustled around in his pack. Then he turned, raising his arm in victory. In his hand, he held two wooden stakes with colored fabric flags nailed to them.

"Are those what I think they are?"

"Yep." Jake beamed with excitement. "I've got two stakes for the race. Now all we've gotta do is get to the land first, hammer in our stakes, file the claim, and the land's ours."

Mason set his coffee cup on a rock near the fire and stood. "How'd you manage to register twice? Isn't that illegal?"

Jake shook his head. "Nope. Not since I signed your name in the registration book for one of them."

"Jake!" Mason hissed. "You got no right signing my name to anything. If Jimmy wasn't so near, I'd be tempted to knock you clear back to Missouri."

"It's no big deal, Mase. All I did was sign your name. Now you can ride with me."

Mason rubbed the back of his neck. "Even if I wanted to ride with you, I don't have a fast horse."

Jake beamed. "Then I guess it's a good thing I've got two."

Mason glanced over to where Jake's two mounts grazed with his four horses. He studied them for a moment. Both looked solid. Long-legged, trim—probably fast. Maybe Jake was finally ready to settle down. If Jake had thought this thing through so well, it might be a sign he had matured—finally.

He sighed, feeling cornered. He could ride for Jimmy and Katie. Getting the land would ensure they would have a home. But they still needed a mother.

"All right. I'll ride." Mason straightened and looked Jake square in the eye. "Under one condition."

Jake's eyes glowed. He smiled the smile that Mason felt sure was the one that had won his sister's heart. "Sure, Mase. Anything. This is the opportunity I've been dreaming about all my life."

Mason closed his eyes, gathering the strength he needed to utter the words that made him sick to his stomach. "I want you to ask Rebekah to marry you and be Jimmy and Katie's mother."

❧

Rebekah stumbled and nearly fell down. She'd forgotten her button box and had come back to fetch it. From the far side of the wagon, she couldn't see the men, but she heard them. "I want you to marry Rebekah. . . ."

If she'd had any doubts about leaving Mason and going to Denver, they suddenly evaporated. She felt as if he had plunged a knife into her heart. He had no way of knowing she'd fallen in love with him. Now he never would.

Holding on to the side of the wagon, she leaned her head against her arm. How could she have been so wrong? She felt certain Mason had feelings for her.

"I can't marry Rebekah," she heard Jake say on a choked gasp.

"Then I can't ride with you."

"Now be reasonable, Mase. I don't love her—I don't even know her."

Bekah eased back behind the wagon. She wanted to run away, but her feet wouldn't budge. With blurred vision, she looked up, checking to be sure Katie was still playing with the neighbor's puppy.

"But she loves the children—and she needs a home. She'll take good care of them and you, too. She's sweet, pretty—sure, she has a temper and can make you madder than a cornered bear, but she's fun to be with. You'll really like her if you just take the time to get to know her. It just makes sense for you two to get together."

Rebekah blinked back her tears as she listened to the words glide on Mason's smooth Southern accent. If he thought all those things about her, why couldn't *he* love her? Maybe she'd pushed him too far—bucked his authority one too many times. If only she could go back and change things. But she hadn't known him back then. She'd been wrong about him. Mason had a heart bigger than the whole West.

"I just don't know, Mase. It seems. . .well, odd, marrying up with someone you don't know."

"Danielle barely knew you when she married you." Rebekah could hear the unspoken censure in Mason's words. "If she'd known you, she never would have married you. I wouldn't have let her."

"Let me think on it a bit, okay?"

"All right, Jake. You've got till noon tomorrow—that's when the race starts, right?"

She didn't hear Jake's response. Fighting back her tears, she tiptoed away from the wagon, her heart in more pieces than a new quilt ready to be assembled. She spied Jimmy playing with Katie and the puppy and numbly moved in their direction. Jimmy gave her an odd look when she asked him to watch Katie for a while. Could he see that she was upset?

She hurried through the field of humanity, desperately looking for someplace she could be alone. People were everywhere. With the big race being held tomorrow, an epidemic of hope and excitement ran rampant throughout the huge tent city. By evening tomorrow, how many of them would feel like she did now—disillusioned, disappointed, their hopes destroyed? All the time she'd been sewing on buttons and repairing clothes to make money, she had hoped deep inside that Mason would ask her not to go. That he would take her west with him—or even better, that they would stay here and make a home near Jimmy and Katie's.

"Hey, lady," a heavyset man in baggy overalls hollered to her. She turned her head, quickly wiping the gathering tears from her eyes. "Yer that Button Bekah lady that fixes shirts, ain't ya?"

She forced a smile and nodded, though thinking about clothing was the last thing on her mind.

"I gots me two shirts that need fixin', and my other pair of overalls gots a hole right in the—" He reached toward his seat then halted his hand and blushed. "Well, they's got a big hole. . .um, well, you'll see."

She couldn't help but smile at his discomfort.

"I'm figuring on gettin' me some land come tomorrow. I don't reckon I'll be back in town fer a while, so I need to get my duds fixed up fore I go. You reckon you could have 'em done before tomorrow? I'll give ya a silver dollar."

A whole dollar. Though she hadn't prayed yet, God was already providing for her again. *Thank You, Lord.* If she had any doubts as to what to do, they just went up in smoke.

She followed the man back to his camp, got his clothing, and arranged to meet him tomorrow, then headed for the train station. Tallying up her funds in her mind, she figured she had close to twelve dollars—thirteen with what she'd make today. That was more money than she'd ever seen in her whole life.

It suddenly dawned on her what the man had called her— Button Bekah. The label brought a soft smile to her face.

In a matter of minutes, Rebekah had purchased her ticket to Wichita. She felt certain she'd have enough money to get to Denver now—maybe even enough to stay in a hotel in Wichita and get her first bath in one of those fancy porcelain bathtubs.

Now all she had to do was figure out how to say good-bye. It would break her heart to leave Jimmy and Katie. For the past few weeks, she'd almost felt like a mother. She'd grown to love them both, but they weren't her children—they didn't belong to her—and wishing wouldn't make it any different.

Then there was Mason. How could she have been so wrong? She'd felt certain Mason was beginning to care for her.

But she must have been wrong.

Growing up in the wilds of Arkansas had not prepared her for dealing with men. She knew she couldn't tell him good-bye without collapsing, so her only other option was to leave while he was riding in the Run. That's what she'd do. Get Ella to watch over the children and she'd be free to leave and chase her dream.

So why was her heart breaking?

seventeen

Mason sat astride the prancing gelding, studying the starting line of the race. As far as he could see in both directions, thousands of people were lined up to the sides and rear, ready to grab a section of free land. Resembling a long, slithering rattlesnake, the line of people, animals, and all manner of vehicles glided back and forth as if it were alive.

Like he and Jake, many folks were mounted on sleek horses bred for speed, while others sat in covered wagons or buckboards filled with all their worldly possessions. A few men dared to venture the untamed land on the back of a contraption they called a bicycle. Mason shook his head, wondering how a man could stay on one of those strange two-wheel ditties.

Give me a horse any day.

The noise was deafening. People yelling, horses neighing, children crying. He wondered how they would ever hear the army bugle indicating the start of the race.

He glanced at his brother-in-law. Jake was more animated than two roosters in a cockfight. He bubbled with excitement over the prospect of winning the land of his dreams. Mason had to admit his excitement was contagious.

He hadn't wanted to ride in the Run, but now he was glad that he'd be a part of history. Win or lose, he would have something to tell his grandkids.

That thought suddenly threw a bucket of cold water on his enthusiasm. Would he ever have grandkids?

Someday. Maybe. But first a man needed a wife.

His thoughts turned to Bekah. Jake had agreed to propose to her if he won his land. All night long, Mason had wrestled with the desire to claim Bekah for his own. If Jake didn't win the land, he'd have no place to call home. Bekah and the kids couldn't live in a tent or hotel room forever. He scouted the land before him. He *had* to get a claim so he could ensure they had a home.

Jake leaned toward him, his eyes twinkling. "Yep, that Rebekah's a fine-looking woman, Mase. She'll be cozy to cuddle up to on a cold winter's night. I'm right glad ya didn't want her for yourself."

Mason's indignation grew. Did Jake have to rub his nose in the fact that he was marrying Bekah? Had Jake actually asked her? And had she said yes?

He closed his eyes and pulled back on the reins to steady his prancing mount. If only he could steady his heart. How could he let Jake marry Bekah? It was time he faced the facts—he was in love with her. He loved Rebekah.

What a fool I've been to push Bekah into Jake's arms. I can't let him marry her. I won't.

Hope soared like the eagle floating lazily in the sky high above him. If he won a plot of land, he could build a home for the two of them—and Jimmy and Katie, if Jake decided not to stay. He could farm the land. It was good land with rolling greens hills, apple trees promising a good fall harvest, plenty of decent-sized creeks that could support a family— though not this sudden influx of thousands of people. The Indians had well-named Oklahoma the *beautiful land*.

In his mind he heard a bugle, then rifle fire and a huge roar. Yanked from his introspection, Mason realized the race had begun. His horse jerked the bit with his teeth and took off like he'd been shot from a cannon. Mason almost lost his seat because his mind had been on Bekah.

"He-yah!" Mason lashed his horse with the reins. Jake was already topping the hill and disappearing over the other side. The roar of the multitude and thunder of hooves echoing across the land matched the throb of his heart in his ears. He would ride for Rebekah. He would win the land; then he'd return and ask her to marry *him*—not Jake.

ꝰ

Rebekah bit back the tears as she watched the huge crowd of home-seekers disappear into a cloud of dust. Mason was out there somewhere, probably at the front of the pack, racing away from her—seeking land he didn't even want.

It had taken a monumental effort to keep a smile on her face all morning when her heart was breaking. Who ever would have thought following her dream would be so painful? Mason had looked at her strangely a couple of times, and she was afraid if he asked what was wrong that she'd burst into tears and tell him how she felt. But it would be too mortifying to tell him of her love only to have him reject her.

She cringed at the looks Jake had given her this morning, like he was already envisioning them married. They reminded her of the same looks Giles Wilbur had given her. How could Mason think she would agree to marry a man she didn't love? Not even for Jimmy and Katie could she do such a thing.

"Are you sure you want to do this?" Ella asked.

Rebekah looked at her friend and nodded. "I have to do this. Mason wants me to marry Jake, but I can't. As much as I love Jimmy and Katie, I won't marry someone I don't love."

"You should marry Mason. Can't imagine what's goin' through that boy's mind for him to tell Jake to marry you. Anyone can tell he's in love with you hisself."

Rebekah shook her head. "You're wrong, Ella. He doesn't love me."

Her things were packed, her train ticket was burning a hole in her pocket, and all that was left was to say good-bye. She knelt in front of the children, studying their cute faces, memorizing every inch.

"But I don't want you to go, Webekah." Katie said, burying her face in Rebekah's shoulder.

"I know, sweetie, but I have to."

"Why can't you stay and be my mommy?" Katie grabbed her around the neck so hard that Rebekah nearly lost her balance.

"It's complicated. I'm not in love with your father, so I can't marry him."

"You could marry Uncle Mason," Jimmy said, his cheeks turning a bright red. "You love him, don't you?"

Rebekah gasped. Were her feelings obvious to everyone? She glanced at Ella. The older woman crossed her arms over her chest. An I-told-you-so grin tilted her thick lips.

"Even if I did, Jimmy, he doesn't love me. You need to have two people who love each other to have a good marriage." She smiled at him and cupped his cheek. "I do love you and Katie, though. I'll never forget you. When I get settled in Denver, I'll write to the post office here—surely by then they will have one—and you can write back to me. Okay?"

Jimmy didn't look too appeased. Katie still clung to her neck for dear life, her tears dampening Rebekah's dress and her tight grasp making it hard to breathe. Rebekah gave Ella a beseeching gaze. The older woman sighed and moved forward, looking disappointed.

"C'mon, kids. Rebekah has a train to catch."

An hour later, Rebekah waved at Ella and the children as the near-empty train lurched out of the station. She grasped the wooden arm of the seat with one hand while pressing the other hand against her churning stomach.

Her heart finally beat normally again after its frantic pace at nearly missing the train. The unimaginable swarm of people getting off when it first arrived had pressed them back away from the station. There had even been people riding on top of the train, clinging perilously to the ventilators. Rebekah, Ella, and the children had been forced to stand under the shade of an old oak tree while the throng of people hurried by, anxiety and hope written on each face—hope that they could still get free land, anxiety that they were too late. She felt thankful that she didn't have to be the one to tell them they were.

Now Rebekah raced toward her own dream: Denver. She felt grateful for the time in big-tent city. Being around so many people allowed her to prepare for the congestion of city life. She felt the same anxiety and hope of those just arriving. Hope for a new beginning—a new home where no one could force her to marry against her will. She felt anxiety over leaving the children. . .and Mason. And she felt concern about what the future held.

She watched the landscape speed by. Trees, bushes, and hills blurred into splotches of green and brown as her eyelids sagged. Worry and thoughts of never seeing Mason again had stolen any hopes of sleep last night. She leaned her head against the seat and closed her eyes. The swaying motion and *clackety-clack* of the rails soothed her like a lullaby as she drifted to sleep with thoughts of what could have been on her mind.

"Miss. . .uh, miss?" She felt a hand shaking her shoulder as she awoke. "Miss, we're coming into Wichita."

"Oh." Rebekah sat up. "Oh, thank you, sir." The thin man smiled and moved on down the aisle. Rebekah picked up her old carpetbag and hugged it to her chest, blinking her eyes to moisten them.

The ticket agent ambled to the front of the coach, rocking back and forth with the sway of the train. "Rock Island Depot, Wichita," he called out, as if she weren't the only person in the whole coach.

Wichita. Why did the name of the town send chills down her back?

Wichita! Curtis's hometown. She straightened in her seat, fighting back a panic that threatened to overpower her. Why hadn't she remembered that?

She turned her gaze toward the city, the first big city she'd ever seen. Rebekah felt her mouth drop as she surveyed the tall buildings and huge houses—some even three stories high. Surely in a town so big, one could go unnoticed. Even if by chance Curtis's family still lived here, they wouldn't know her. She'd never met any of them. And Curtis had no reason to think she'd come here. She drew in a slow, steadying breath. Things would be okay.

Minutes later, the train screeched and groaned as it pulled to a stop at the Rock Island Depot. She covered her face, hoping to block the unpleasant odor of the coal plume streaming from the engine. Her clothes were hopelessly covered with a gritty layer of soot.

Gathering her courage, she stood and followed the ticket agent to the door and down the three steep steps to the wooden platform. For the first time in her life, she was in Kansas. Even the massive tent city she'd just left hadn't prepared her for the enormous town of Wichita. She took a breath and looked around, spotting the ticket booth after a few moments.

Making her way through the waiting crowd, she finally reached her goal. She waited in line, listening to the conversations around her. Over and over, she heard the Land Run mentioned. She sincerely hoped all these people weren't wasting their money on a ticket there.

She'd heard Wichita was a big cow town, and as she looked around, she saw evidence of the Western influence. Cowboys dressed in denim and boots stood next to men in fancy three-piece suits. Occasionally she caught a whiff of the stockyards when the wind gusted.

Half an hour later, Rebekah sat on the bed in her room in the Occidental Hotel, probably the biggest structure she'd seen so far. The whole three-story building was built of brick, and huge, white pillars supported the ten arches along the front. She'd never imagined staying in a place so fancy. The little house in the backwoods of Arkansas paled in comparison to this fine place.

The brocade bedspread, the color of ripe wild raspberries, matched the ceiling-to-floor draperies. An ivory-colored desk with an opulent chair sat between the room's two windows. A small divan and two end tables rested along the wall across from the bed. Never in her life had she seen anything so luxurious.

As amazing as the room was, Rebekah had a hard time enjoying it. Though her body wasn't in Oklahoma anymore, her heart certainly was. Yawning, she eased onto the fancy bed and closed her eyes. Thinking back over the last few weeks, she breathed a prayer of thanks. "Thank You, God, for keeping me safe on the trail and for sending Mason to watch out for me. Thank You for showing me how to make the money I needed. Please show me how to deal with the pain of losing Mason and the children. Keep them safe, Lord."

Like lemonade without enough sugar, the words left a sour taste on her tongue. "What's wrong with me?" She pulled a fluffy pillow out from under the bedspread and tucked it under her head. Tears blurred her vision. Instead of facing Mason and telling him how she felt about him, she'd taken the coward's way out and run away—again.

Mason would be furious with her. But why? Why would it matter if she were gone? He probably didn't care. He'd be happy to be rid of her. Immediately she felt guilty and shook those thoughts from her head. Mason may not love her like she did him, but she knew he cared what happened to her. It was his way. He might be gruff and bossy at times, but in his heart, he was a caring person.

So what now?

The words she'd heard out on the trail reverberated in her mind.

"Go back."

"No, I can't. Don't ask that of me." She wrapped the pillow around her head as if to keep the words at bay.

Why had she ran from Mason this time when she'd stood up to him so many other times? She knew the answer. She couldn't stand to find out he didn't love her. But wasn't it better to know for sure than to wonder the rest of her life? "What do I do, Lord?"

"Go back."

Rebekah sat up and wiped her tears. Resolve was winning the battle over doubt.

"I can do all things through Christ which strengtheneth me."
The words from the Bible seeped into her mind, filling her
with warmth like a cup of hot coffee. The only way she'd
have peace and be able to set up a new home was to know
the truth. She had to face Mason, tell him how she felt, and
see if he felt the same.

She reached in her pocket, fingering the ticket to Denver.
In her mind, she calculated how much money she had left.
If she was very careful, she could go back to Oklahoma and
still have enough money to make it to Denver. She'd arrive
penniless, but she could worry about that when she got there.

That's what she'd do. She'd go back and face Mason—one
more time.

❧

Mason rode slowly back into town. Both he and his horse
were exhausted after riding all day in search of a plot of land
that hadn't already been claimed by those sneaky Sooners.
Time and again, he thought he'd found unclaimed land,
only to end up with a rifle in his face, urging him to look
somewhere else.

He'd tried to keep up with Jake, but after spotting him
riding over that first hill, Mason had lost him in the swarm
of racers. The directions Jake had given him to the land he
wanted weren't as clear in reality as they had been when Jake
first drew them in the dirt by their campsite. Mason sincerely
hoped Jake had secured his land.

He rubbed the back of his neck as he guided his horse
back to camp. Already the town looked much different. The
population had shrunk enormously, and now there seemed
to be mostly women and children left behind while their
men raced for their future. Pieces of broken wagons littered
the initial race area. It looked as if some people's dreams had
died before they'd gotten out of town.

For a time, he'd allowed himself to get caught up in the
excitement of Jake's scheme. If he'd won a claim, he could
have asked Rebekah to marry him, and they could have

settled there. But what now?

Mason didn't like feeling as if he'd failed. He didn't know how to deal with failure. All his adult life, except for when his wife had died, he'd pretty much been able to control things around him—other than the weather.

The smell of fresh-cooked beans and salt pork tickled his stomach as he rode into camp. He couldn't wait to hug the children—and Rebekah. The thought of her waiting for him wrapped around him like a warm blanket on a chilly night. When had he fallen in love with her? When he'd found her helpless on the trail? When she'd stood in his face, refusing to allow him to tell her what to do? He didn't know when; he just knew it had happened. ·

His gaze searched the campsite as he dismounted. He wondered where everyone was. His mount's head sagged with exhaustion as Mason removed the saddle and rubbed him down. The horse was a fine animal. Maybe he'd see if Jake would swap him for a couple of his draft horses. A decent saddle horse would suit him better on his trip west than one of the big, slow-moving horses. But was he still going west? No, not unless Rebekah would go with him—he knew that much.

"Uncle Mason!"

He spun around to see Jimmy running toward him, closely followed by Katie. Both children looked upset—red eyed, as if they'd been crying. Mason squatted so he could look them in the face. "What's wrong, pardner?"

"Rebekah's gone. She left on the train."

eighteen

Rebekah was gone?

The words crashed into Mason as if the locomotive had physically run him down.

A tearful Katie crawled up into his lap. Standing, he tucked her to his chest as Jimmy wrapped his arms around Mason's waist. He hadn't seen the children this upset since their mother died.

"When?" he whispered, his voice cracking.

"This morning," Jimmy said, wiping his damp face against Mason's stomach.

"Why did she leave?" It hurt him more than he could say to know she'd run away again.

"She—she didn't want to marry Pa." Jimmy looked up at him. "She said two people had to love each other for a good marriage to work—and she doesn't love Pa."

She knew about his crazy suggestion for her to marry Jake? How?

He gritted his teeth. He knew why she'd ran away. Rebekah surely felt he was pushing her into an unwanted marriage to Jake just like Curtis had tried to force her to marry that Wilbur guy. A sharp pain gutted his midsection. How could he have done that to her?

"She wuvs us," Katie said as she raised her head off his shoulder, rubbing a fist in one of her damp eyes. Her little face was splotched with red—obviously she'd been crying a lot today. "She wuvs you but not Pa."

Mason blinked. Rebekah loved him? How could Katie know that?

"What makes you think that?"

"Ella said so," Jimmy offered. "She told Rebekah she

159

should stay here and marry you 'cuz she loves you."

A tiny smile tilted Mason's lips in spite of his concern. "What did she say then?" he couldn't help asking.

"Webekah said you don't wuv her. Is that true, Unca Mathon?" Katie looked at him with her big, watery blue eyes. She wiped her nose on her sleeve and stared at him with childish innocence, waiting for his answer.

"Well, do you?" Jimmy asked.

"That's what I'd like to know, too." Mason glanced up to see Ella standing there with her arms crossed over her ample bosom.

"Well, uh. . .yes, I do love her." He straightened, feeling more confident now that he'd voiced the words out loud.

"Good. That's what I thought. So what you gonna do about it? Just gonna let her run off, or are you going after her?" Ella pinned him with that matronly glare of hers, making him feel like a naughty schoolboy.

"I'm going after her." He glared back then kissed Katie's cheek.

"Weally?" Katie asked, wide-eyed. "You gonna bring Webekah back?"

"Yeah, I am." Determinedly, he set Katie down. "Where'd she go, Ella?"

"Wichita. You're gonna need to eat first." She hurried toward her campfire. "Won't do to have you passin' out from hunger."

An hour later with his belly filled with beans and corn bread, Mason headed for the train station as he breathed a prayer. "Lord, I need Your help to find Rebekah. Wichita is a big town."

Mason stopped dead in his tracks. He'd actually uttered another prayer—and it felt good. He moved off the road and sat down on a pile of lumber.

He yanked off his hat and rubbed his head. Before he could face Rebekah, Mason had bigger fish to fry.

"Dear God, You know I've been angry with You for a while. Sorry 'bout that. I nearly died when You took Annie and Danielle from me. Okay, sorry, I know You didn't take them. I'm sorry for blamin' You. Please forgive me. Lord, help me to make things right with Rebekah. Don't let me lose her, too. And thanks for being patient with me."

He blew out a cleansing breath and smiled. It felt good to be right with the Lord again. He'd stayed away too long. Mason stood and started jogging toward the train depot.

"Mase!" Jake called. Mason pulled to a halt and turned to see Jake running toward him. "I did it, Mase. Got that purty little quarter section I told you about. What happened with you? Did you get any land?"

Mason shook his head. "No luck, I'm afraid. Everywhere I went some Sooner was already setting up camp."

"I'm real sorry about that. But I did it!" Jake grabbed Mason around the neck and gave him a brotherly hug. He couldn't help but smile. If Jake felt this happy, maybe he'd settle down and be a decent father. "Never had such luck—"

A shot rang out. Mason jumped as Jake slumped against him, his eyes registering complete shock. "Got me, Mase." His words slurred together as his body slid down the length of Mason's. He tried to hold him up, but the dead weight pulled him down with Jake.

Mason jerked around to see where the shot had come from, hoping he wasn't next to get a bullet in the back. A skinny old man with a smoking pistol was being overpowered and wrestled to the ground by a group of men. "That varmint stole my land," he yelled.

"Hang on, Jake." Mason hugged his brother-in-law to his chest, feeling the liquid warmth of blood on the hand that cradled Jake's back. "Someone get a doctor!"

"Too late," Jake wheezed. He pushed slightly till he was away from Mason's chest. Slowly, he reached inside his vest and withdrew a rolled-up piece of paper.

"Yours." Jake fought to lift his arm but lacked the strength. It dropped to his chest. "Take it," Jake whispered. Mason held Jake with one arm and took the paper. "Take care of my kids, Mase. You always were—a better father—than me."

Jake labored to take one more breath; then his eyes and head lulled back as he released the sigh of death.

"No!" Mason roared. "This wasn't how things were supposed to be."

"C'mon, Mason." His mind slowly registered Luther's deep voice speaking to him. A warm hand squeezed his shoulder. "Jake's gone." Mason glanced up to see Luther's concerned face peering down at him. "Nothing you can do here. Ella says you got a train ta catch."

Mason laid Jake on the ground and stood, feeling the deep grief of a wasted life. Moments before his death, Jake seemed to have finally found the one thing that satisfied him—this land. *This stupid land!* Mason wanted to scream. *Was it worth dying for?*

Mason shook his head and unrolled the parchment—the deed to Jake's 160 acres of land. Something wasn't right. Mason closed his eyes tightly, then opened them and stared at the paper again. It was a deed all right, but the name on the deed was Mason Danfield, not Jake Conners.

He glanced at his brother-in-law's silent body. Why had Jake done this? Had he known he wouldn't be any happier tending this patch of land than he had the other places he'd once called home? Jake had seemed so happy. Was his happiness brought on by the fact he'd given the land he'd wanted so badly to Mason?

Mason knew those questions would remain unanswered. He knelt beside Jake's body, wondering what to do. There were things that Jake might have for his children. A watch, a bit of money, but Mason didn't have the heart to rummage through the man's vest. It had to be done, though. He reached out with his fingers twitching in hesitation.

Luther cupped his shoulder. "You go on now, son. I'll tend to Jake. You go get that little lady and bring her back to us. Me and Ella will watch your young'uns till you git back."

Mason nodded woodenly. He took a final look at his brother-in-law and numbly moved toward the train depot.

He wanted to be mad at God, but Jake had made his own choices. Jake knew about God—Danielle had made certain of that. In the end, everyone must make up his own mind about God. Jake had made the wrong choice, and now he'd live all eternity with his decision.

Instead of being angry with God, Mason embraced Him even more. If nothing else, Jake's death had reinforced the truth about how short and precious life was.

The train whistle sounded, cutting into his thoughts. He broke into a run. He had to make that train. His whole future depended on it.

❧

Now that her mind was made up to return, Rebekah felt at peace. She'd enjoyed her luxurious bath, thankful for the warm, clear water. Last night's dinner had been scrumptious. Not stew or deer or half-burned biscuits but tender roasted beef and potatoes with dinner rolls. And this morning's breakfast had been a masterpiece. She licked her lips and sighed at the memory.

There was also much to be said about the glory of beds; she'd slept soundly for the first time in weeks. Walking back to the train depot, the town didn't seem quite as intimidating as it had yesterday.

She smiled, wondering what Mason's expression would be when he saw her again. Rebekah nibbled her lip. Would he be angry that she'd run off when his back was turned? She knew he didn't like how she kept running from her problems instead of facing them head-on. Mason had probably never run from a fight in his life. Well, this time she wasn't running. She'd come face-to-face with her problem and see what his response was.

"There she is! I told you I saw her."

Rebekah stopped dead in her tracks and turned her head at the familiar voice.

No, it couldn't be. Not when she was so close to realizing her dream.

"Well, lookee here, Giles. If it ain't my lovely runaway

daughter." Curtis Bailey's words dripped with undisguised hatred. "You really put us through the ringer, girl. You're gonna be real sorry."

Rebekah was already sorry. Giles Wilbur and her stepfather stood in her path. Her heart felt like it had lodged itself in her throat. Her gaze darted in every direction, searching for an escape.

"Ain't nowhere to run." Curtis grabbed one arm while Giles latched on to the other. She realized the two men had picked the only spot between the hotel and the train depot where they could have overpowered her without a crowd noticing. She never should have tried to take a shortcut through the alley. They pulled her toward two scraggly horses tied up at the other end of the alley.

"No, I won't go. I can't." Rebekah jerked her arms, hoping to get free. *Please, God, help me. Don't let this happen.*

"Ain't no use fightin' it, pumpkin. Your pa and me had a deal. You're mine now."

Rampant fear like she'd never known before raced up Rebekah's spine. She struggled against their firm grip, her body wrenching and tugging till her arms hurt.

"You can't do this. It isn't right."

"What ain't right is your runnin' off when I had me a business deal with Giles." Curtis slid a look her direction that could curdle milk.

Rebekah's fine breakfast roiled in her stomach. Is that all she was to him? A piece of property to be traded at his whim? She wouldn't go willingly. She kicked him in the ankle. When Curtis's steps faltered, she booted Giles's ankle, too. Both men spat out foul words, but Curtis turned toward her with his hand raised. Ducking her head, Rebekah braced herself for the blow.

"I wouldn't do that if I were you."

Mason!

Still struggling against her captors, Rebekah peered over her shoulder. Mason's smooth Southern voice was like a balm, but it was the look on his handsome face and the pistol in his hand that gave her hope.

"Let her go," he hissed. The muscle in his jaw twitched, and she knew he was angry. She only hoped none of his anger was directed at her.

"Stay out of this, mister. You're not a part of this," Curtis yelled back.

"You're wrong there," Mason said.

Giles and Curtis spun Rebekah around so they could face Mason. With eyes narrowed and that gun in his hand, he looked like a gunfighter.

"How you figure, stranger? This here's my girl, and he's the man she's marrying." Curtis jerked his thumb toward Giles.

"Nope," Mason said, shaking his head. "You're wrong."

Curtis and Giles still maintained their death grips; her wrists throbbed.

"Wrong 'bout what?" Curtis crinkled his brows in a stern glare.

"Well, the way I hear it, you're not Rebekah's pa, and I know for a fact that he's not the man she's marrying." Mason pointed his pistol at Giles, and the man slunk back as if trying to get out of range.

"What makes you say that?" By now, Mason had obviously stirred up Curtis's curiosity. Rebekah was beginning to wonder what he meant herself. Glancing past him, she felt a small amount of relief when she noticed the crowd gathering at the end of the alley. Maybe someone would help them.

"I know she's not marrying that ol' coot because she's marrying me." Mason cast her a glance, almost daring her to disagree.

Hope burgeoned within her, but tinges of doubt soon followed. Was he just saying that to save her, or did he really want to marry her? He pulled his gaze from hers and refocused on her captors.

"Look, I don't want to shoot either one of you. But if you don't let Bekah go right now, I will."

Giles looked at Curtis. "Much as I want your gal to come live with me, I don't want to git killed over her. Look, you can keep that half side of beef I swapped for her, but I want my moonshine back."

Rebekah closed her eyes. Could she be humiliated any further?

"I ain't giving you back that moonshine. Look at all the money I spent helpin' you look for her."

Giles slowly released his grip. "I didn't force you to come. You wanted to. You said no girl was—"

"I know what I said," Curtis hollered back.

Giles gave Curtis a shove. "I want my moonshine back." Curtis stumbled, releasing Rebekah's wrist, and fell to the ground. Lumbering back to his feet, Curtis took a swing at Giles. Rebekah crept back against the alley wall toward Mason just as the sheriff and two deputies rounded the corner.

Instantly the sheriff pulled his gun. He eyed the two men wrestling in the street, then pointed his gun at Mason, who still had his pistol drawn.

"No," Rebekah screamed. She raced toward Mason and threw herself in front of him.

"Now just hold on, missy, and move away. I don't want you to get hurt," the sheriff said.

"You don't understand, sir. He was rescuing me." She pointed at Curtis and Giles, who still tussled in the dirty alley, kicking up dust and yelling a string of expletives. "Those men tried to kidnap me."

"That's right, sir. I was only trying to save her."

Rebekah heard Mason holster his gun then felt his warmth as he wrapped his arm around her waist and pulled her back against his chest. The sheriff cast him a studious gaze as if trying to decide if he was holding her against her will. Rebekah didn't hesitate. She turned and wrapped her arms around his waist.

Thank You, Lord.

"Bekah," he whispered into her hair. "I thought I'd lost you."

"Me, too," she cried into his chest. "Me, too."

Mason held her tight. The noises behind her faded as she realized that being in Mason's arms was the fulfillment of all her dreams. She didn't need to go to Denver. Everything she needed and wanted was right here. If only he really wanted her.

"Shhh, it's okay. You're safe now." Mason kissed her head and tightened his grip on her.

"Uh, miss?" she heard the sheriff say. Rebekah turned her head, staying in Mason's arms, and peered at the tall man. "I'll need you to come to my office and make a statement."

"Yes, sir," Mason answered for her. "Just give her a few moments to calm down."

She heard the sheriff give Mason directions to his office and watched as he and his deputies marched Curtis and Giles away. The crowd seemed to follow, and in a few moments, she and Mason were alone in the alley.

Rebekah buried her face in his chest, afraid now that he'd scold her for running away and getting herself into this mess.

"Bekah?" Mason whispered against her hair. "Are you okay, sugar?"

She nodded against his shirt.

"Look at me."

Rebekah released her hold on Mason's waist and leaned back. He loosened his grip only enough so that she could look up into his face. His expression took her breath away.

"I meant what I said. I want you to be my wife."

A gasp caught in Rebekah's throat. Could she dare hope he was serious? "Why?" she squeaked.

"You know, don't you?" Mason smiled, and a butterfly war was loosed in her belly.

Rebekah shook her head. Mason glared teasingly at her.

"I think you do know." He lowered his face to hers, stopping to gaze deeply into her eyes. His eyelids lowered as his lips touched hers. She wrapped her arms around his neck, hoping this moment would never end. Mason truly wanted to marry her.

"Why do you want to marry me?" she murmured against his warm lips after a few moments.

"I love you, Bekah. Can't you tell?" He deepened his kiss, pulling her tighter against his chest.

He loved her. Rebekah couldn't seem to grasp it. He really loved her. But she still had unanswered questions.

She pulled back and waited for his eyes to open. His onyx gaze burned with love and promise, but she still had to know one thing. "What about Annie?"

Mason closed his eyes for a moment. "Annie's dead. She'll always be a part of me, but she's my past." He opened his eyes and captured her gaze. Leaning forward, he rested his forehead against hers. "You're my future."

Rebekah's heart leaped for joy. He *was* serious. Somehow he'd put his wife's death behind him.

"I've made my peace with God, in case you're wondering." A sweet smile graced his lips; then his eyes twinkled. "Any more questions?"

Rebekah bit the inside of her cheek. Mason raised his hand and ran his knuckles down her jawline. She nodded. "What about Jake? Why did you want me to marry him?"

Mason's gaze darkened. "I'm sorry you overheard that. Very sorry. Guess I just went loco for a while." He flashed her an embarrassed grin. Then his smile faded.

"What is it?" she asked, cupping his stubbly cheek.

Raw hurt glittered in those dark eyes, and he looked away. "Jake's dead."

Rebekah sucked in a stunned breath. "How?"

"Shot. Some ol'-timer thought he'd cheated him out of his claim."

"Did he?" Somehow she could see Jake doing something like that. Instantly she felt guilty for thinking bad of the dead.

"I don't know. It doesn't matter anyway. The old man will probably hang for shooting Jake in the back just for a little piece of land."

"Oh, Mason, I'm so sorry." Rebekah leaned against his

chest and hugged him with all her might. "Those poor kids. What will happen to Jimmy and Katie?" Even before she uttered the words, she knew the answer. Mason would take care of them—just as he'd taken care of her.

"Looks like I'm gonna be a daddy after all." His soft chuckle resonated across his chest, tickling her cheek. "You reckon you're ready to be a momma?"

She leaned back, looking into his handsome face. She still needed to hear three little words again before she could answer that.

As if reading her hesitation, he said, "Ah, sugar, can't you tell I'm crazy in love with you?"

Rebekah couldn't hold back her grin. "It's about time," she said.

Smiling, Mason pulled her back into his arms and thoroughly kissed her again. "I'm still waiting for an answer," he said on a breathless whisper. "Will you marry me?"

"Yes! Oh, yes."

"Wahoo!" Mason yelled.

Standing on her tiptoes, Rebekah lassoed his neck with her arms, hugging him until her toes began to hurt. Finally, she dropped back down and looked around, realizing what a spectacle they were making.

She gazed up at the man she loved with all her heart and remembered her mama's words. *"Sooner or later, some handsome man is going to sweep you off your feet and make you his wife."*

Her mother's words rang true. Soon, very soon, she would be a wife and a mother.

Mason smiled down at her, obviously wondering what was going through her mind. She smiled back at him. Taking his cheeks in her hands, she rose up and placed a kiss on his soft, warm lips. "Let's go get our kids—just as soon as we finish with the sheriff. All right?"

"Yes, let's. But first, how about if we visit a minister?"

Rebekah smiled. Mason wasn't one to waste time once a decision was made.

"Don't you want to wait so Jimmy and Katie can be there?"

"No, I'm not taking a chance. It would be my luck to get you back to the tent city only to find out all the ministers have left town."

"Okay."

"Okay?" He eyed her with suspicion. "You never give in this easily."

"You've never made me such a generous offer before." With a coy smile, she batted her eyelashes at him.

Mason's laugh echoed through the alley. "All right, sugar, I'd better be happy winning this battle so easily. Don't expect I'll be so lucky in the future."

"Shall we, Mr. Danfield?" Rebekah held out her hand to him. With a smile that warmed her insides more than a campfire on a cold night, Mason took her hand and headed toward the street.

Rebekah looked up at the bright blue sky and smiled. She'd found a family to love and one that loved her. She knew in her heart that she'd never be on the run again. She was home.

A Letter To Our Readers

Dear Reader:

In order that we might better contribute to your reading enjoyment, we would appreciate your taking a few minutes to respond to the following questions. We welcome your comments and read each form and letter we receive. When completed, please return to the following:

Fiction Editor
Heartsong Presents
PO Box 719
Uhrichsville, Ohio 44683

1. Did you enjoy reading *Sooner or Later* by Vickie McDonough?
   ❑ Very much! I would like to see more books by this author!
   ❑ Moderately. I would have enjoyed it more if

   _____

   _____

   _____

2. Are you a member of **Heartsong Presents**? ❑ Yes ❑ No
   If no, where did you purchase this book? _____

   _____

3. How would you rate, on a scale from 1 (poor) to 5 (superior), the cover design? _____

4. On a scale from 1 (poor) to 10 (superior), please rate the following elements.

   ____ Heroine   ____ Plot
   ____ Hero   ____ Inspirational theme
   ____ Setting   ____ Secondary characters

5. These characters were special because? _____

_____

_____

6. How has this book inspired your life? _____

_____

_____

7. What settings would you like to see covered in future
   Heartsong Presents books? _____

_____

_____

8. What are some inspirational themes you would like to see
   treated in future books? _____

_____

_____

9. Would you be interested in reading other **Heartsong
   Presents** titles? ❏ Yes ❏ No

10. Please check your age range:
      ❏ Under 18   ❏ 18-24
      ❏ 25-34   ❏ 35-45
      ❏ 46-55   ❏ Over 55

Name _____

Occupation _____

Address _____

City, State, Zip _____

Presents

Great Inspirational Romance at a Great Price!

Heartsong Presents books are inspirational romances in contemporary and historical settings, designed to give you an enjoyable, spirit-lifting reading experience. You can choose wonderfully written titles from some of today's best authors like Peggy Darty, Sally Laity, DiAnn Mills, Colleen L. Reece, Debra White Smith, and many others.

When ordering quantities less than twelve, above titles are $2.97 each.
Not all titles may be available at time of order.